A TALE OF THE NORTHLAND REBELLION
IN THE AGE OF THE BLACK SUN

ORPHANS &
OUTCASTS

ORPHANS &
OUTCASTS

We are all but dust in the wind
At the mercy of Fate
Which turns the Wheels of Time
Until the day we harness the wind
Become more than dust
And Queens of our own Fates

A TALE OF THE NORTHLAND REBELLION
IN THE AGE OF THE BLACK SUN

Book One
Northland Rebellion

PUBLISHER
Kylie Leane

COVER ARTIST
Ben Wootten

COVER LAYOUT
Kylie Leane

ORPHANS AND OUTCASTS

PUBLICATION HISTORY
Paperback Edition / November 2017 Kylie Leane
ISBN: 978-0-9944382-3-2

For information address:
authorkylieleane@gmail.com

Kylie Leane can be found online at
authorkylie.com

Other Works By Kylie Leane

Chronicles of the Children
KEY: Book One
Protectors: Book Two

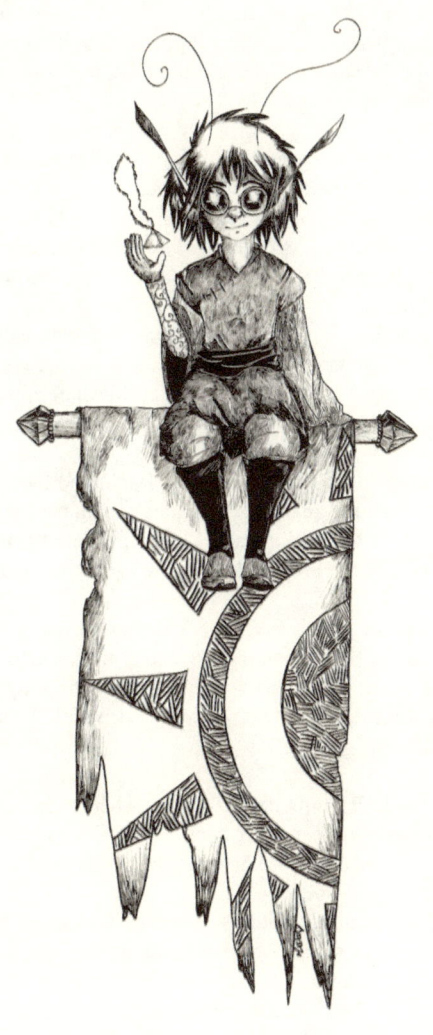

IN MEMORY OF
Lance

Thank you for being my Denvy,
Your tales are missed.

SCRIBE'S NOTE

Thank you, Readers, for waiting patiently for another book.

I'm really grateful for all the support throughout the journey of writing, illustrating and publishing. I hope I can continue to bring you wonderful tales.

I'm going to take a moment to explain how *Northland Rebellion* fits into the world of *Chronicles of the Children*.

Chronicles of the Children is the 'Main Series' – however it is a huge epic. I started realising I wasn't going to be able to tell every facet of the story within the main series since I am only following the main characters through their journey.

Chronicles of the Children and *Northland Rebellion* will occasionally intersect, with characters traversing back and forth between each series. I've been writing the books in the hope that they'll be read side-by-side, complimenting each other, someday.

When I was a little girl I was always fascinated by the idea of the characters who couldn't go on the great quest, who held the castle while the heroes went off to fight in wars. What was their story? What if the heroes never returned? How would they deal with the situation?

That is what the *Northland Rebellion* was born out of, the desire to know the tale of the secondary characters who remain behind. The wonderful characters who keep the candle burning brightly. Waiting with the hope that, someday, their heroes will return and having to become heroes themselves.

Can you read *Orphans and Outcasts* without having read *KEY* or *Protectors*? Yep. You can start here if you like and work your way backwards. I'll be curious to see how that works for you.

A word of thanks to my editor, Elle. She took what was a rough stone and polished it until it shone. I cannot thank her enough for the months of hard work she puts into editing my dyslexic mayhem.

A huge thanks to Ben Wootten for another stunning front cover. I love it, I adore it, and it's everything I dreamed it to be.

I am always grateful to my parents for their ongoing support, much of it emotional, and my sister, Mel, for our many hours of conversations.

Finally – to you – dearest readers. A thank you, to all of you who read, review, and who follow me on Facebook and Twitter. You've been a part of this journey. Thanks.

Enjoy the tale!

Your scribe,
KL

THE BLESSING

You look like you have had a rough trip, friend?
The burning-sea can be feisty to new travellers, I'll give you that.
Mayhap you need a beverage,
a stool to rest your feet after a weary journey?

I can enlighten you with a tale as you linger.
Nay, it is not a sailor's tale, friend.
This is a tale of truth and those who sought it,
For the seeking of truth is often the beginning of great heroism.

Our world is but one of many,
Folded over each other,
like sheet upon sheet,
Layer upon layer,
As many as the grains of sands in the burning-sea.
Each unique.

But they all have one thing in common—
The Song of Eternity

Only in some worlds does the Song take shape.
Our world is one of them.
You travel in a special world.

Lawless child
nyhot class

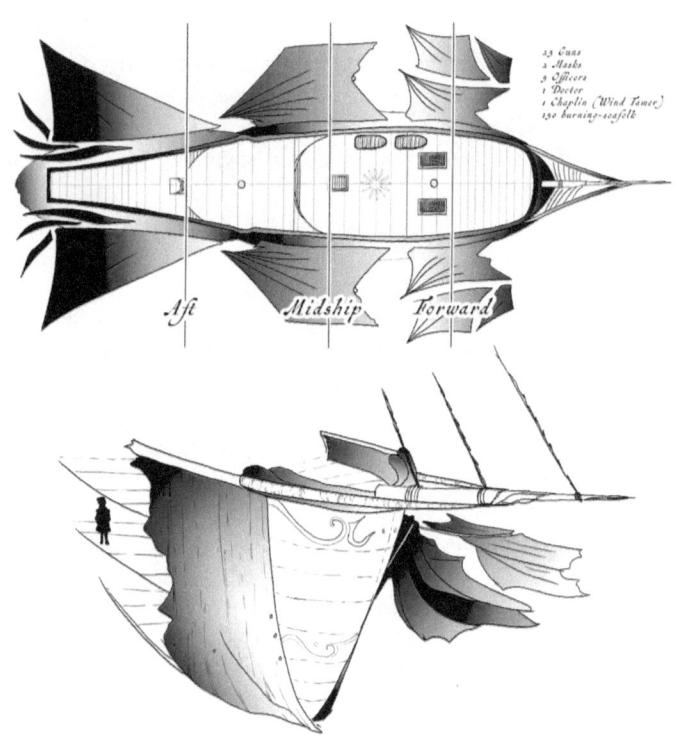

15 Guns
2 Masks
5 Officers
1 Doctor
1 Chaplin (Wind Tamer)
150 burning-seafolk

Aft   Midship   Forward

AALDRYN SILVERTIDE & KHAMSIN

CHAPTER ONE

There is nothing left.
Kemet is gone. Kemet is gone. How could we have allowed this to
happen?
Had we truly grown so complacent in ourselves that we believed we
were invulnerable?
We believed we had tamed a Dragon—(why, why did they not listen
to you? Why did they not slay it?)
I sit here, my dearest Sekhmet, surrounded by the mirrors that reflect
my failures.
What have we done?
Kemet is gone.
There is nothing left.

Private Communications Link.
Utillian Time 14:19PM.
Signal: Strong.
Upload: Completed.
Do you wish to send?

Aaldryn dashed across the sand, the fine grains roasting his foot-paws despite them never touching the surface for longer than a moment. The wind sang a howling song in his ears as he raced Utillia's wide skylines. In the distance the bow of the Lawless Child crashed down, cutting its way through the mighty sand-waves like a blade. The Sun, low behind the dunes, was a herald of the coming Twin Winter months. The cooling air from the higher dune shadows tangled between his legs, dulling the heat of the scorching sand. A school of juttfli cackled and jittered around him, their oxygen holes bursting with billows as they leapt sky-seaward in sparkling hues, only to vanish into the mysterious realm below.

These precious moments of freedom were just for him and Khamsin. The wind-god who dwelt within him cherished the running of the burning-sea. In these few scarce hours they were one in mind, lost in the immensity of the horizon.

It has been a good day. The wind-god stroked the filaments of his awareness. It was not so much a voice that he heard but a sensation of lingering like an old etching carved into stone, for Khamsin was as ancient as the Ovin-tu Mountains[1] and always it felt as though he was a call echoing off distant cliffs.

"Indeed," Aaldryn replied. "I hope we uncover something in that

---

1   The mountain range that rings the borders of Pennadot.

null-zone. Thanks be to the Rythrya[2], maybe we'll finally get enough funds to upgrade the generators."

A horn hollered, spiking his pelt. Thick lines were flung over the edge of the *Lawless Child*, breaking the waves. Aaldryn breathed deeply through his air-gills. A thrill chilled his under-pelt as he watched the sand-ship spreading her outer wings. She was not an overly large vessel—a nyhot class[3], crewing only a hundred and fifty able-bodied burning-seafolk—but she did them proud and he adored her almost as much as he adored his mate.

He dropped to all fours, increasing his speed. The wind surged around him, spurring his body forth with leaps and bounds until he latched onto a rope, clawing up the hull with strong hauls. With a flip, he twirled into the air and landed with an expert swagger on the decking. He caught the movement of the sand-ship as he stood upright on his hind-paws. His fan-tail unfurled, steadying his posture.

The two upper-decks of the sand-ship were busy with scurrying crew members, obeying the orders of the queen, all paying him no heed despite his rank of chaplain. The vessel shuddered under his foot-paws as the *Lawless Child* took the brunt of a strong gravity swell, thrusting out from the null-zone beyond.

They were vagabonds and orphans, cast-offs from the Ruling Prides, drawn to the *Lawless Child* for the same reasons—protection, shelter, food, work—a home, a pride. To the unobservant it was not so obvious, but to his eyes it was easy to see those who were unique like himself—the misfit-born, cursed with mutations caused by the rising radiation leaking free of the null-zones and the Zaprex technology beneath the burning-sea.

In many ways it was better to be dead than to be born a misfit. Whether Human, Kelib, Kattamont or half-breed, the shame was a cutting blade and life within the Ruling Prides was impossible.

Aaldryn curled his extra digits into the hooks of his dangling belts. The scars had long been hidden by his silver pelt, but he could still feel them pull from time to time, reminding him of his childish attempts to cut off what he had once considered an abomination.

Through the commotion a commanding voice called, "Prince Aaldryn, get your tail up here! Report!" Aaldryn caught sight of his mother aloft the stern deck: Zafiashid Silvertide, exiled queen of the

---

2   Rythrya – means 'Guiding Stone'. In this case it is in reference to the 'Seven Rythrya' which are the great guiding stones worshipped in Utillia by all Kattamonts. However, scattered across Utillia, there are many 'rythrya' used to guide sand-ships through the burning-sea. Chaplains use them to navigate the winds and currents.

3   Nyhot – medium sized sailing vessel, two masts. Typically equipped with twenty-five guns, five officers, a doctor, chaplain (wind-tamer), purser, and up to one-hundred and fifty able-bodied burning-seafolk.

Silvertide Pride. The glow of the Sun was raw behind her, casting a glinting halo around her glossy unkempt fur. She was dainty behind the heavy weight of the helm, the magnificent contraption of wheels and levers dwarfing her in size, and yet there was no doubting the queen's prowess.

She might have been an exile of the burning-sea, cast aside like trash by the Silvertide Pride that ruled the Trading Routes between the Wind Cities and Isles, but her queenly strength was unwavering. Like raw silver, pure from the ground, she had been born to rule the strongest pride of Utillia, and that air of royalty had never left. It was something she had passed to him, in the way he sashayed up the stairs to the helm. She did not glance his way as he stationed himself directly beside her, but her flamboyant air-gills briefly flashed in greeting and, within, Khamsin berated him sharply for forgetting Kattamont customs.

Zafiashid cared not that she mingled with the low-life scoundrels of the outlaw trading posts, or the criminals and pirates that winged through the outer sectors. That, he knew, was true pride—that she had been outcast but had never lost what she had been born to be.

"Mother, I scouted ahead and the null-zone is over the next wave-bank. Nixlye was correct in her dreamings; there is a ruin inside."

Zafiashid spun the wheel, locking a lever in place with a foot-paw. Her tail balanced her weight as she guided herself around the controls. "Good, good. Does it look like anyone has discovered it already?"

"It looks unscavenged."

"All the better; we shall be the first." Her grin grew wild, bright azure eyes ravaging the horizon yonder in anticipation. She did so love the hunt. Aaldryn swished his fan-tail lazily, envious of the colours his mother's had; it glinted like a precious opal, while his had the pristine blues of scarce water. Mother had never told him why she had been outcast, but he had gathered enough over the sol-cycles. It had been because she had birthed a misfit. It perhaps explained the intense drive he had inherited to search for and learn more of the Zaprexes, following in her unwavering paw-steps.

What truly lay beneath the burning-sea? Wonders untold—long uncharted cities, sunken and left to slumber. He had barely scratched the surface of their great towers in his countless dives. They called to him. He had to follow. It was because he was misfit-born, and all misfit-born shared in common the dream of the cities paved in gold.

Mother knew he craved answers. That was why they had become archaeologists. It was a dangerous profession; they were labelled heretics by the Iposti—a formidable rival pride—for their beliefs that the Zaprexes were not invaders but saviours. He was not afraid of being branded a heretic, but what he truly despised was the dirt they had to put up with to fund their research. For the upkeep of the *Lawless*

Child and food for the crew, they were forced to allow Scavengers to use the sand-ship and accompany them on exhibitions.

It went against everything an archaeologist upheld to tolerate Scavengers pulling apart the wonders of a Zaprex ruin. He felt filthy just thinking about it.

"Must they come, Mother? This is truly a marvellous find and they will destroy it."

Zafiashid's brow lifted under the linkage of her air-gills. Aaldryn unfolded his arms, spreading them in protest.

"And, yes, I detest the man." He spat.

"It is simply your pride instinct. Resist it."

"I want to stab him in the face whenever I see him."

Her laughter rang high into the Mist sails. "That is what you get for being born a pure-blooded prince."

"Mother!"

He had been born a prince, and the prince's place in a pride was to protect. Queens and princesses lived for the hunt. Aaldryn stiffened as he caught the scent of the leader of the Scavengers. Zafiashid was smiling and he rolled his eyes, feeling his fur spike as the heavy footstep of the Human thumped up to the helm. There was no way he was going to duplicate his mother's gesture of greeting towards Torka. The stinky Human could go throw himself overboard for all he cared.

"Greetings, Queen Zafiashid! I see we have been in luck and found some fair winds."

Zafiashid cocked her head toward him and Aaldryn shrugged nonchalantly. He might have given Khamsin free range to push the *Lawless Child* along; it was not a bad thing to have a wind-god permanently residing within his mortal shell—he was personally going to take every advantage it brought. After all, he was the sand-ship's chaplain; taming the wind was his role on the vessel—the Pride had just never seen fit to inform the Scavengers about Khamsin. To the vultures he was, quite simply, a very good wind-tamer and he did so enjoy how much it vexed them.

"Indeed, Torka, the Rythrya Stones have smiled upon us."

The Stones do not cause the winds. Your mother needs to remember who it is that truly rules these oceans. Khamsin stirred, bristling under his fur like hot-fire. Aaldryn snorted, insulted on behalf of Khamsin for being compared to the monuments scattered around Utillia.

"Mother, the Rythrya are guide stones, nothing more. They do not create the winds." Aaldryn glanced over the tossing dunes in the distance. "The Simoon forge the winds."

"Ever the scholar, Aaldryn," Torka said. "You fill your head with useless facts from a useless past."

Torka's bass laugh was heavily weighted with a gurgling of tobacco use. It was never a good thing for a Human to abuse their lungs in

Utillia—the air was already too thin for a first-generation Human of Pennadotian birth.

"The past is not useless, Torka," Aaldryn muttered. "It is from the past that the future shall be reborn." He could not understand how anyone who dived deep into the burning-sea, down into the depths of the Zaprex wonders below, could not see that the rebirth of their world was beginning. Aaldryn unfolded himself from his perch, levelling the man with a glare. "Besides, it is my useless facts that bring you coinage to fill your useless pockets." He had not encountered many Humans Torka's age; most who sailed the burning-sea died before they had the chance to reach more than fifty sol-cycles. He was not entirely sure if Humans could get much older. Half-breeds he had encountered—they had many amongst the crew—but pure Humans usually remained in the Wind Cities and the Isles, preferring the life of mist-farming or trading. Torka, though, was beginning to go gray and he smelt of foul decay that was off-putting. His long hair was always bound back, and he often wore a broad smile as though life was pleasant. His skin had long since seen better days, wrinkled and blotched by the boiling Sun and the radiating burning-sea. Yet it was still the smirk that Aaldryn detested the most—so smug and self-satisfied, like he knew something no one else did, some grand secret he was content to let sit on his lips but never to tell.

"I think what the prince is trying to say, Torka, is that the ruin is un-scavenged. If you and your men will prepare for the dive, I will get close enough to drop you off."

"This is good news Queen Zafiashid. My men have been holding out for a good bit of scavenging."

"I hope this will be fulfilling for us all." Zafiashid heaved on a lever and the vessel beneath them lurched forward. Aaldryn steadied himself as a side-wing caught an up-gust of gravity and he seized a nearby handle, throwing his full weight upon it.

He bellowed over the deck, "Tie down that wing! Why is it still open? Someone tie that cursed thing down. We're closing on a null-zone. The gravity is destabilizing. I want the wings buckled down."

Zafiashid laughed and he shot her a glare, fluffing the fur of his chest in frustration. "I would be grateful, Mother, if you took better care of the sand-ship I will inherit when you cross the Osiris Gate."

"You will not inherit it, my prince. Your queen will."

"It will still be my sand-ship."

Torka cracked a laugh. "Maybe we might find your queen some legs this time, heh, boy. Some records did say those Zaprexes could rebuild limbs better than our Kattamont mechanics."

Aaldryn quenched Khamsin's internal raging tornado. The indecency of the Human man was beyond insulting. It was enough to justify cleaving his head from his shoulders and putting it on a stake. Had this been any other Pride, he would have.

"I will prepare myself for the dive, Mother." Aaldryn turned sharply, his fan-tail coiled irritably. Maybe if he had wind-blessed luck, Torka would take a bad fall this scavenger hunt and never come back up. After all, the burning-sea took no prisoners. He heard his mother's laughter as he stomped away. It was troubling, though; he was not entirely sure if he was happier to be away from Torka or his mother.

Neither his mate nor his blood-brother were in their cabin, their usual hiding place from the crew of the Pride. Aaldryn breathed in their lingering scents. It calmed his nerves. Collecting his assortment of archaeological and dive equipment from a locked chest he donned the hand-crafted belts and foot-paw pads and snatched up the face-mask. It was a ghastly thing, made all the more uncomfortable by the tubes that attached to his air-gills, but the presence of toxins could be possible in any ancient Zaprex ruin, and that could not be taken lightly, even by a Kattamont. He had seen Humans melt when exposed to spores and gases below the surface of the burning-sea.

He headed topside. Zafiashid's voice was shrill over the groaning of the *Lawless Child* and the bustling of the crew as they anchored the sand-ship on the edge of a high dune wave. Khamsin's spirit soared through him and Aaldryn breathed out deeply, sensing the delight of the wind-god as its tentacles danced around the metal of something beyond his sight. They had found it—something old, and yet it felt impossibly new and undamaged by the passage of time and the burning-sea.

Aaldryn sighted Nixlye on the deck leaning over the railing. Her tail poked through a hole in her wheelchair, flapping in a clear display of joy. He smiled. For a half-breed, his mate leant more toward a Kattamont nature, and for that he was eternally grateful. Her Humanness was in her peculiar hands and her cute little nose. She had none of the magnificent Kattamont air-gills but had at least inherited a tail and fur. She was already a queen, though she pretended otherwise for the sake of their Pride unity and his mother's sanity—though neither queen would admit it to the other.

At the death of a queen, such as his Pride mother, the waiting neutral princess would mature and take her place, inheriting the Pride, including the princes and neutrals under her rule. His mother was not dead; she was an outcast, staying alive by her sheer desire to win back the honour she had lost. Nixlye was not a neutral princess, but, out of deference to his mother, she kept the façade as his mother's princess. He was sure this was only possible because his mate was half-Human and their Pride was one of misfits. It was the part of her that was Human that did not mind being a second queen to his mother.

After all, in truth, it was his mother who suffered—she had no princes, no one to care for her; she was alone—like a rythrya stone amongst the sand dune waves, weathering the storms of the burning-sea's rage.

Nixlye was the true queen; the shadow queen his blood-brother would often say.

With stubby ears twitching, she caught his stare. The glow of her rosy fur brightened at his admiring gaze.

"Ryn!"

He smiled at her shortened version of his name. It bothered his mother, which was perhaps the reason both his blood-brother and his mate used it so often.

"Oh, Ryn, isn't it beautiful! I wish I could go with you."

His chest ached as she rolled the wheels of her chair around. Under the patchwork blanket of her own making, he knew her legs lay limp. Only he and his blood-brother had the privilege of seeing her uncovered. His mate was strong, not only in spirit, but also in body. Her life was one of tribulation. He had been childish, thinking his little extra digits were a blight on his life. Nixlye had still been in the womb-sack of a female, and, due to the mutation of her bones, her legs had never developed correctly. It pained him to think that were it not for the softened heart of one Iposti she would not be alive to love him.

He hooked his extra digits into his belts and levitated over the deck, landing beside her in a swell of wind.

"If the Human oafs were not coming I would take you, love."

"You shouldn't speak ill of Torka; he is a nice man. Besides, I am half-Human, so you should be kinder to my people." Nixlye fluffed her chest fur, settling back in her chair.

Aaldryn rolled his eyes. Nixlye's insistence on acknowledging her Human side extended to wearing Human clothing, which was bothersome to get off her at night, and it ruined her adorable rosy pelt. Why keep fur as luxuriant as his mother's under that much fabric? He did not see the point. Kattamont fur was supposed to be without restriction; otherwise it did not absorb sunlight or starlight—but, no, Nixlye refused to listen to his nattering on the subject.

"You're judging me; I can feel it." She eyed him.

"I'm undressing you in my head," he sniped back.

Her tail thumped him, causing him to stagger forward, more in surprise than at the force of her strike. He caught her cocky grin and the shine of her mottled blue eyes.

"Find me something, Ryn. Bring me back a gift."

She so loved the beautiful wonders they uncovered, the artefacts of centuries past that her fingers could touch and her mind process. He promised himself he would find something for her to cherish, just to see her happiness.

The wheels of her chair grated over the deck and her hands grasped the surface of the railing. Nixlye stared wistfully over the horizon. "Be safe, too," she murmured.

"I will, I promise." The adventure of discovery was thrilling, but it was still dangerous. Even with all the caverns of secret wonders, the possibility of finding clues as to why Utillia existed as a land of scorching irrational sand, there always remained the danger he might not return from below. He had been raised a warrior-scribe, and he would always seek the answers, despite the risks.

Aaldryn fluttered a soft breath of wind across Nixlye cheek, causing her to laugh as she tucked her hair behind a perky ear.

"I can feel it, Ryn." She tipped her head toward him. "I don't know what it is, but I know we're getting closer to the source of our dreams. We'll figure it out—what happened to us."

She was speaking about his extra digits, his mutation, and how she even existed at all—half-breeds—they should have been impossible.

He did not know which was sadder: the fact that his mate believed unswervingly in the Zaprexes or that, no matter how much they searched, they never came any closer to that which all misfits dreamed of—the cities of gold.

Aaldryn bent and nuzzled her cheek. "I trust our dreams. They have carried us this far."

"As do I."

Aaldryn straightened at Zafiashid's low voice. He stepped aside from Nixlye sharply, bowing to the queen.

"There is an island nearby; we shall dock there and await your return. It is far too dangerous to keep the *Lawless* this close to a null-zone; we could destabilize the gravity and collapse the area onto you while you dive." Zafiashid approached, brushing a paw through Nixlye's hair tenderly. Aaldryn curled his foot-claws against the wooden planking.

"Yes, Mother."

"Then you have your orders, prince. Come back alive."

"Always." He sent a swell of wind toward Nixlye to caress her cheek as he turned and skipped over the edge of the sand-ship into the burning-sea below.

01001011 01100101 01111001

One of Aaldryn's great pleasures in life was annoying Torka with his ability to walk on the burning-sea without sinking. Only skilled Iposti chaplains could do this, and the fact that he, a young prince, flaunted it, irked the Human scavenger to no end. He could tell from the twitching of Torka's eyebrow and the way his lips curved into thin lines. The man loathed him, and the feeling was well returned in kind.

The surging pulses of the destabilizing gravity of the null-zone made his fur spike. He would never get used to the sheer power that Zaprex technology radiated, nor come to understand how and why pockets of emptiness would open up within the burning-sea and leave vast sectors unstable. Some burning-seafolk called them *holes*, but they were not holes in the term of a visible gap one could swing a rope into and drop down into the dark depths. It was an area of no sand, no burning-sea, just nothing—appearing suddenly and without warning in a sector. They could be big or small. If they occurred when a sand-ship was nearby, or right beneath a sand-ship...well, he had seen it happen from a distance and it was never pretty.

Somewhere in the pocket of nothing lay a Zaprex machine, a wonder of extraordinary history just waiting for him. Waiting for him to discover why the null-zone existed and why Utillia had become a land of moving sand, why misfit-children were born, and why the world they lived upon was crumbling, piece by piece.

"What do you think we'll find down there, cub?"

He glanced at Torka as the man strapped his booster pack to his hips. While he did detest the Human, he had to grudgingly admire him for being the best in the scavenging business.

Aaldryn fitted his mask, attaching the tubes to his air-gills.

"The null-zone is small, so I suspect it won't be a city entrance."

Torka nodded. "Good, good. Last time we got a city entrance I lost three men."

Aaldryn shuddered. Ah. Yes. That had not been a good hunt. The crystal-spores from the Zaprex corpses had been particularly lethal, and they had gone down so far, and so deep, he had almost expected to never resurface.

He had been glad Torka had been unable to scavenge the Zaprex remains due to the spores. Desecrating the fairy-kin's castles felt disrespectful enough, let alone taking the hollow bodies for spare parts.

"It is unlikely that will happen this time, Torka." Aaldryn shook his head. "But I do suggest caution. I suspect we will encounter some crystals, so full protective gear if any of you want to father children."

"You heard the cub!" Torka shouted to his men, "Don't mess up your suits this time!"

"Why doesn't he wear one?"

Aaldryn glanced back at the questioner, giving the new-comer a smile as he stepped over the edge of the null-zone.

"I'm already tainted. Misfit-born, remember."

"It's why he's here, numbskull. He can sense the shiny-crystals and warn you not to step your foot in it." Torka whacked the young man over the head and Aaldryn smiled as he released Khamsin, beginning his dive. It was disorientating, as he knew he was going downward, but there was no reference point for the slow movement when all around him was entirely *nothing*. When he had first begun his expeditions into null-zones he had thought his eyes were playing tricks, catching signs of life, trickles of sand, and whiffs of light. He had tried to reach out and catch the strange fragments only for them to break up and disintegrate in his paws. Khamsin called it corrupted information and now whenever he took the plunge into the odd world of nothing he knew that surrounding him was not mere darkness but a lack of anything at all. It made him feel very alone, very empty, and even more frightened of the world he lived in. The burn of the scavenger crew's booster-packs glittered, and he watched them pan out, creating a formation. Torka swirled around him; finally the man was in his element. Aaldryn eyed the booster-pack, wondering how easy it would be to accidently kick Torka hard enough for the booster-pack to grow unstable—

Aaldryn, I have promised to protect all *the lives upon the* Lawless Child, *and that includes Torka. If you desire to fight him, you will have to do it as a Kattamont prince with a grudge, then mayhap I will aid you with throwing him overboard. Currently, the man has done nothing to slight you but ruffle your kitten feathers.*

Aaldryn winced at Khamsin's berating.

"You are no fun," he muttered.

Faint light appeared below them. Aaldryn glanced up, shaking his head at the sight of the small sliver of daylight some distance above. Despite how long he felt the dive was, they had not truly travelled far. On his deepest dive he had reached the sixth level, which, despite the great depth, only gained them access to the very tops of the ancient Zaprex cityscape, and that alone had taken days to achieve. They had barely broken the surface during this dive. He looked at Torka. Honestly, he should get along with the Human he spent so much time diving with.

Torka manoeuvred his booster-pack controls, swinging towards him, his cheeks flushed rosy against the burn of the pack. "Any idea what it is, cub?"

Aaldryn squinted. This close he could finally make out the shape of the old Zaprex monument. His chest inflated sharply with surprise. This was a spectacular find. If only his mate and blood-brother were with him. He could imagine their delight.

"A flying machine." He barely managed the words.

Torka clapped his hands. "Oh, oh!" The scavenger whirled back around to his men. "Lads! We got ourselves the catch of the sol-cycle."

It must have crashed here. Khamsin nudged his mind. *It is strange.*

Aaldryn frowned. Yes, it was strange—the way the eerie shape was suspended in the nothing, globs of sand surrounding it. Crystals were scattered, as though they had been shattered when the null-zone had been created. Others protruded through the hull of the ancient vessel in such a painful manner it made him cringe. He could only liken it to a pin-cushion from his blood-brother's healing kit. The crystals' glow was an allure though, drawing him closer as a moth to a flame.

There is something inside. Something different. Something…new…

"What?" Aaldryn raised his brow. "Really?" His tail flicked. New was good.

Khamsin's wind rippled over his fur. *Sometimes, young one, it is not always good. The wind is the element of change, and not all change is good change.*

"*Tah.*" Aaldryn waved aside the wind-god's concern. "We will bring Nixlye back a grand treasure."

JARVIS OF THE PLAINS PEOPLE

CHAPTER TWO

Beloved Nefertem of mine,
Why do you sit surrounded by mirrors that reflect your failures?
Do you not see the greatness I do—do you not see the inventor,
the scientist, the coder, the life giver?
Beloved Nefertem of mine,
Your mirrors lie to you;
Kemet is not gone;
Kemet lives in you.
As long as your Song remains, and your Dynasty walks upon this
world,
Kemet lives on.

NORTHERN TOWER – PRIVATE COMMUNICATION LINKAGE –

01010011 01100101 01101011 01101000 01101101 01100101 01110100

Jarvis breathed in deeply, his heart pounding. No matter how much he tried to calm his nerves, thick darkness still made him sick with fever. The shivering was uncontrollable despite the dense humidity of the hot, tight confines. He painted the world outside his tightly shut eyes through the tiny electric particles drifting around him, sending sparks of information through his skull, down his spine, and into the receptors spread across his skin. His tussle with a Zaprex machine had resulted in philepcon liquid contaminating his system, but he had adapted, slowly integrating it into his body. He rather liked the comforting feedback loop of extrasensory information that fed through to him from outside sources.

The steel wall at his back was slick with his own perspiration and blood. Even his heavy breathing contributed to the moisture in the air, making his downward climb slow.

It was not the first time he cursed his growing body. Wynnilas might not be the stockiest of Human breeds, but his recent grow-spurt and rigorous training had filled out what had once been skeletally-thin limbs. If only he had kept his skinny boyish body for a while longer, this tight squeeze down an air-vent of a Zaprex star-glider might have been an easier adventure. What was his master thinking? He was supposed to be avoiding all contact with Zaprex technology, not diving head-long into some ancient vessel, rich with fairy-life.

He could sense it in the walls, a breathing of life that was waiting for long lost owners to return. Just as philepcon liquid flowed through his veins, so it silently swelled through the fortifications of the living ship, singing the melody of the dying world itself—a song he had picked up miles away and brought to Master Titus' attention.

Titus may have been eccentric, wild like the wolves of the Ovin-tu Mountains, but he had a brilliance that Jarvis admired deeply. When he had told the Messenger Hunter about the possible Zaprex vessel buried in the burning-sea his first thought had been to use it to throw a signal to the House of Flames and warn them of Coltarian's impending eruption—to evacuate—or as his master had so eloquently put it, *'to get their* totus *out now!'*. Yet was any place safe to flee to, really, when the Dragon's return was fated? Khwaja Denvy, for whom Titus had great respect, was convinced the Dragon's minions were up to something in Utillia, something that involved the ancient Zaprex technology. Though surely the old lion could not know for certain what had been occurring in a land he had not walked upon for centuries—even if that land was his homeland.

Jarvis felt his chest swell. Without him to use the Zaprex technology, Master Titus would never have considered delving into such a dangerous place. He might not know why he had ended up a Changeling, his body slowly being converted by the philepcon liquid he had been infected with, but he was convinced there was a reason for his current state.

He was going to do everything he could to help. As Messengers did what was directly before them, to the best of their abilities, so would he. Khwaja Denvy had grumbled and said a few of Titus' more colourful Trench words before letting him accompany his master into the Zaprex ruin. The problem with having Zaprex technology living inside flesh was the inability to determine what it was doing. He could sense Khwaja Denvy's concern for his well-being…and yet they were all more worried about Khwaja Denvy's deteriorating health.

"Itsy bitsy spider went up the water spout." Titus' voice was muffled somewhat by the tight confines of the air-ducks.

Jarvis' hands were sweating, smearing their oddly blue-tinged illumed perspiration on the glossy walls he struggled to cling to. His master, somewhere below, continued to sing the old children's tune that was now looping in his head.

"Itsy bitsy spider went up the water spout. Down came the rain, and flushed poor spider out."

"Master Titus, that is not helping!" Jarvis shouted into the gloom. He squeaked as his boots slipped and he plummeted, losing control of his gravity-bubble as fear of the unknown overwhelmed him. Skin burned as he fought for a grip, smashing his fists and heels against the walls until he stopped. His racing heart thrust daggers through his chest and he stared blankly into the humid air, tasting his own blood.

Cursed Sun On High, he was being so childish, not controlling his own gravity and not keeping his thoughts stable.

"Jarvis? Yeh all right up there, laddie?"

Come to think of it, how, by the Almighty Sun, was Titus doing this? His master was a fair bit larger than he was. Then again the Messenger had been consumed by a Twizel; it would not surprise him if he had simply turned into some kind of slinky shape and slid down the walls. Jarvis groaned. Oh—how far he had come from the farms of his forefathers.

"Fine. I'm fine. Just having trouble stabilizing my gravity. I think it might be, ah…It might be the dark and the humidity."

"Ah, yah, it could be left over conditioning from yer imprisonment. Don' let it get to yeh. Happens to the best of us. Yeh should have seen me before I was consumed. Piece of stinking pve'pt poop I was. We be almost through, I think. I can see a light."

Jarvis found Titus' nattering relaxing. His imprisonment haunted him—the torture of the Twizels that had slaughtered his family, the lashes that still scarred his flesh. But if Titus mentioned it, somehow it did not seem so frightening. Titus had an odd way of making him feel respected despite still being a lad. According to the Hunter, in the eyes of Messengers, at ten and three sol-cycles he was old enough to run his own squadron. Titus looked to him to hold every type of responsibility a Messenger his age would, whether he had been trained in the legendary House of Flames or not.

Apparently his ordeal of being captured and kept in a box for two sol-cycles warranted respect from his master. He was not about to lose that respect now.

Hand under hand, he continued his downward climb.

Titus was right, he concluded, peering at the symbols floating in front of his vision: they were almost through the network of small tunnels, per the data that trickled into his mind from the new environment around him.

"Ah-hah!"

The shout of victory tickled his alerted ears. Jarvis winced at the high-pitched twang and shook his head, trying to rid himself of the echo.

"Made it! Come on laddie, ain't too much further ta go. Drop—yer gravity will catch yeh."

"I can't."

"Jarvis, trust yerself. Trust yer gravity. Come on, Little Weasel. When Zinkx was yer age he infiltrated a Zaprex Way Station and took down eight of the machines inside."

"Zinkx this, Zinkx that!" Jarvis spat back. "All you and Khwaja Denvy do is talk about how amazing Sir Zinkx is. I'm starting to think he doesn't even exist."

A bellowed laugh caught him by surprise. "I'll give yeh a clue, as long as yeh don' tell Clive. He truly does think Zinkx is as grand as we make him out ta be. What be better, laddie? The story of a grand legend, or the truth of that grand legend? What if the truth of that legend be a nightmare? Be it not better to tell a fabricated fairy-tale?"

"I would rather the truth."

"Yah, yer be a spoilsport, Little Weasel."

"Stop calling me that!"

"Oh, I made yeh mad. Get down here and punch me."

Jarvis hissed. He dropped. Gravity control had taken him months to perfect, and he had needed it to manage Ki'b, the little Kelib girl who had claimed him as her future husband. Whatever would his mother and sister have thought of him, betrothed so young like a little lord of a lofty city? His father would have laughed like a jolly old drunkard. With the cheerful thought of his family's smiling faces foremost in his mind, Jarvis sailed downwards, daring to speed up until he caught a glimmer of light and abruptly halted himself inches from the floor.

Titus whistled and clapped. Jarvis cocked his head to one side, looking across at his master leaning casually against the wall. Whenever he heard Titus' drawling voice he imagined a tall melanite-skinned Southern Tempath from the silver mines with a pick-axe over his shoulder. But Titus was not a Tempath; he was a Retenna breed—skin like yellow orthoclase, hair as fierce as the fires of their cities' furnaces, and a body as spindly as the willow trees that lined the mighty Cor River Network. Titus was not his voice.

"Khwaja Denvy says I must refrain from showing anger." Jarvis straightened his tattered leather vesting. Ki'b was going to be upset again over the damage to it. She fretted something awful about their attire, now that they could afford to buy clothes again.

"If Khwaja Denvy told yeh ta walk off a cliff, would yeh do it?"

"No."

"Good. Just checking." Titus ruffled his hair playfully. He pointed down a dark corridor. "I say let's go this way."

Jarvis rolled his eyes, visualising the direction with his optical view of the star-glider's schematics. Holographic symbols, invisible to Titus, spun around him as he walked beside his master. The world was lit in a brilliant display of images and he cringed at his inability to translate Zaprex. He was able to comprehend certain things due to the new information feeding into his mind, but he could not understand the language. It was as if he was missing a vital key. His fingers coiled unconsciously around a small prism tucked under his vest. The hum resonating from the piece of crystal was a constant comfort.

"Well, I gotta hand it ta the fairies—they had some nice decorations," Titus called from up ahead. Jarvis caught up, finding him admiring a section of crystals that had burst through the corridor floor and twisted into a formation around the ceiling.

Titus' hand reached out for the dazzling glow and Jarvis reacted instinctively, pulling his hand aside.

"Don't touch, Master! They are not normal crystals!"

Titus looked at him in confusion.

"They are the Matrix Crystal of this vessel," he quickly explained, releasing the grasp on Titus' wrist. "I think, from what I am picking up from the mainframe, this ship crashed here, and it was never shut down properly. No one was here to look after it, so the Matrix Crystal broke out of confinement and it has bled through into the other systems. If you touch it, it will send out a charge…oh…"

A smile had snaked its way across Titus' lips and Jarvis groaned, rubbing a hand through his hair in frustration.

"Right, you're technically already dead. I forget that."

"Nice that yeh do, laddie." A grateful wink was cast his way. It was true; Titus did like it when any of them forgot about what he called his 'untimely burden', so he could be poetic and embellish his tale for later retelling.

"Just wanted ta see if it be the same as the ones in the House of Flames." Titus held his hand closer to the light of crystal. Jarvis watched in morbid curiosity as his master's skin peeled back, and, layer by layer, the flesh decayed until all that remained was bone. Titus rattled the bones playfully, wiggling his eyebrows boyishly.

"Shouldna be surprised, I suppose. I be a creature of shadows and Zaprexes loved their light."

"I'm sorry, Master."

"Aw, don' be, Little Weasel. I stopped bein' sorry about it a long time ago." His hair was ruffled by the cold bone hand.

"What does it do? Do you know?"

Titus gave a thoughtful tip of his head. "Hmm, I think it is the form of light the crystals give off. It is on the same spectrum as the Sun or some mumbo jumbo like that, blah, blah…I never listened to Raphael long enough to keep up with what she was saying." Titus studied his burning skin for a brief moment longer before unhooking his magnificent black coat. He wrapped it around his frame. The silky fabric activated upon meeting his shoulders and pooled, protectively coating him.

"Happened all the time at the House, with them *thraki* crystals hanging everywhere," Titus muttered. "One of the many reasons why I was decommissioned ta Second Base. The High Elder said I made people uncomfortable, being what I am and all."

"But you're not a Twizel. Surely they understood that?"

"Messenger society is jaded, laddie. Had I not been the one ta've been turned, I would have acted just as they did. Yeh only see the world different when yeh step outside of the world. Remember that."

His master tapped his forehead sharply and Jarvis winced.

"This noggin of yers is too good ta waste. That's one thing yeh do have in common with the real Zinkx."

Jarvis smiled. "The *real* Zinkx."

"Aye, the one who doesn't kill Twizels with his bare hands." Titus cracked a laugh. "That's what I do. Ohhh, wait until you run into Graa-crels, or Mites, or worse…Brainny-suckers."

"Brainny-Suckers?"

"Yes, Brainny-Suckers are their official name in the Library. We tend to shorten it to Suckers, though, yeh know, 'cause yelling 'Brain-ny-Sucker!' takes a wee bit long." Titus held up two fingers. "That's with two Ns, by the way. Very important that."

"You're making this up."

"No, mah son named them. Don' let kids name monsters."

"Just out of curiosity, what is your son's name?"

Titus turned a corner, throwing back a grin in his direction. "Rosie Red Telvon—after his great, great, great grandfather General Richard the Red, who slaughtered the Magnificent Graa-crel in the Battle of Purification."

Jarvis smiled. During his imprisonment by the Twizels, and the long two sol-cycles in a wooden cage, he had come to understand that Messengers cared very deeply about the historical tales of their past. Even if the stories they told were comically overdone to the point of myth, they had a wonderful sense of grandeur to them.

Messengers lived in their past, Khwaja Denvy had said, because they did not believe in a future. They had fought the same endless war for so long, they no longer saw anything more than war and now he, Jarvis of the Plains People, had become part of the Messenger mythology.

He passed mutated crystals, each filled with philepcon liquid that resonated a song to which his own heart was beginning to rhythmi-cally time itself.

"Sir, we should take the next right. I think the control deck is down that corridor." Images scattered over his vision as he looked back and forth, scanning the lower decks. The creaking of the hull was grating on him, just as much as it grated on the star-glider. The poor vessel was very tired—tired of lying in the sand-sea, being subjected to the pull and push of the haywire gravity, and controlled by the tides of Utillia. He felt sorry for it, to have been left all alone, dying, with no one to hear its silent screaming.

"I can hear you," he whispered. "I can."

Titus nodded. "Lead the way, Little Weasel."

He still could not understand why Titus had decided on Weasel for his pet name. He certainly did not look like one. If anything, his annoying adoptive sibling Clive was more of a weasel than he was, but

Titus had named Clive 'Volcanic-Boy' for his eruptive behaviour. That was no better, and he could not understand why Messengers had to come up with random, stupid names for each other—or maybe that was just a quirk of Master Titus.

He huffed, wedging his hands into his hip-bags.

A door ahead of them had been jammed open by a large crystal formation, growing up the side of the wall and spilling out into a flower shape. Jarvis smiled, wishing Ki'b was with him, she would have loved the beautiful sight more than anything. Dropping onto his knees, he slipped under the ancient growth into the wide expanses of a round Central Control Room. His chest expanded as he breathed in the purified air, still ventilated through the star-glider's inner core. Many of the floating terminals had collapsed from their stations, but a few remained free-standing. He skipped over to the upper-deck, landing elegantly on the main boulevard.

"It must have been something when it was fully operational."

"We're here for a reason, Jarvis, not ta explore ancient wonders. The last time yeh did that yeh got yerself infected. Let's hurry this along. I don' like the feeling in the air."

Jarvis pouted. Why did no one else feel what he felt whenever they approached Zaprex ruins—the songs that lingered sorrowfully, waiting to be set free? It was all so sad, and beautiful at the same time.

He brushed a hand against a panel, static coursing through his finger-tips.

"Hello, *Bez-at:_Who_Lingers_by_Water*." He chuckled as the vessel's name trickled over his optical lenses. "It is an honour to meet you. I hope you don't mind, but I'm going to tap into your mainframe."

He wanted to laugh aloud as a garbled reply fizzled over his optical lenses. So, the star-glider's computer, while in hibernation, still maintained enough of a personality to respond. His heart was flooded with an incredible swelling of connection as he settled into a floating glossy chair. The moment he contacted the surface of the seat, the interior of the room ignited with life. Titus yelped in alarm.

"What'd yeh do?"

"Don't worry. It's just sensing the philepcon liquid in my body. It isn't enough to fully restart the ship, but I should be able to tap into the base-level programs. I'd need to be a full hybrid or a Zaprex with actual code to run this ship on my own. My philepcon levels are still too low right now for me to be classified as a hybrid. Give it some more time though, I'm sure."

"When did yeh grow an extra head?"

"When I got infected by a fairy-machine. You remember it don't you, Master?" he joked mockingly. "You lopped off its legs and smashed its heart while I was there. I thought I had died."

"Aw, yeh wee Little Weasel. Scared of dying, are yeh?"

Jarvis raised an eyebrow. "I dunno. I guess."

"Yah, well, someday it happens ta us all. Just depends on how. Personally," Titus put a long knife to his own throat, "I'm hoping for a swift chop to the neck."

"Fitting." Jarvis rolled his eyes. It was another thing he had learnt in the company of Titus. Messengers discussed death and the passing to the Glorious Sun as though it were a common occurrence. He supposed to a race of soldiers it was, but it had been confronting to adapt to both Khwaja Denvy's and Titus' indifferent outlook on death. Even now, Khwaja Denvy facing his end, when he had once been an immortal, did not seem to cause alarm.

It felt as though it should.

A god dying in the way Khwaja Denvy was—it felt disrespectful.

At least Ki'b was making a fuss, but, then, she was Kelib, and she respected ancient traditions.

He shook his head. He had become a Messenger, but it did not mean he had to think like one. He was still Jarvis of the Plains People.

Unhooking the triangle pendant from around his neck, he slotted it into a section in the terminal. Holographic screens ignited, spreading around him and he searched through them. So many words he had yet to learn. The language tumbled into his mind, but he could not comprehend it. It was far too much for him to currently grasp; it was all one step at a time. He flicked aside the seemingly useless information and kept a single display.

"So, we are sending a message out on a loop, right?" Jarvis glanced over his shoulder.

Titus paced the room irritably.

"Aye, aye. If yeh can do it."

Something had spooked the Hunter, though he was not letting on what it was. Jarvis' neck hairs hackled as he twirled a holographic control. He tugged up his sleeve, reading the scrawled-out numbers Khwaja Denvy had given him that morning.

His brow furrowed as the screen glittered red, the symbols blurring. "Are you sure this code is correct, Master? It is registering as very old and, considering the state of this ship, anything it considers old must be, well, ancient. Guess I'll just backdoor my way in."

"It is old because Duamutef may well be the oldest thing I know, and, thus far, it has never changed its base-code, so it should be the same." Titus' black shape settled beside him, resting like a hawk. "If yeh tap into its mainframe, the signal will boost itself, hopefully. At some point it will figure it out, if it ain't too busy running around after idiots."

Jarvis fiddled with the nearest loop, cocking his head as he listened to the static noise over the ancient crystal-wave network. With a Matrix Crystal that had bled out of its containment, they should have managed to extend the signal. Neither he nor Titus needed to worry about the repercussions of the contamination that came with spending too long exposed to a naked Matrix Crystal.

His body was becoming metal and crystal, and Titus was dead—but he dreaded to think of what was happening to those who dwelt in Utillia.

"Who is Duamutef?" he asked.

Titus was silent. It was never a good sign when his master was silent. Titus was either talking or stalking around but rarely did he grow silent unless a problematic question was asked or he was under pressure.

"Duamutef is the Lady of the Tower."

Jarvis crinkled his brow. "What?"

"Yeh know—the Towers! The brilliant thingy-ma-bobs that are supposed to fuse the *jarvik* world together."

"I know what the Towers are," Jarvis shot back with a glare. "It's just…why is it a lady of them? Wait. You kept calling it an *it*... Why not a *she* if she's a Lady?"

Titus raised an eyebrow. "Yeh be the one turning into a Zaprex machine, standing in a Zaprex flying contraption. Should yeh not know the answer to that question?"

"I should?"

"Aye."

He could not think how this was relevant, and the expression on his face must have revealed his confusion as he heard his master chuckle. He returned to his work, tapping a few more keys on the terminal, listening to the gentle hum of *Bez-at:_Who_Lingers_by_Water's* hibernating song.

His eyes widened and he jerked back to look at Titus. "*Lady_Duamutef:_of_the_Tower*! It's a princess-ship. That's how you address a princess-class sky-ship. You're telling me I am trying to contact a princess-class sky-ship?" His chest swelled in sudden overwhelming excitement that such an old relic could exist.

Titus made a 'so-so' gesture.

"No? Not an AI?" Jarvis frowned. "But…"

"Tell me." Titus bent forward. "Would yeh give yer protector bot a different personality?"

His jaw went slack. His protector bot. The machine that had infected him, that was now invading his flesh and slowly, piece by piece, consuming him. Sometimes he could feel it there, floating like a random thought in the back of his mind, or an ignored chore he might have dismissed on his father's farm. He knew it was there, a part of him now, but it was dangerous.

"I suppose it does have a different personality."

"Does it have a name?"

"It has a designated code, yes." Jarvis frowned. "What does this

21

have to do with Duamutef?"

"As a hybrid yeh've made the distinction between the two factions within yer mind. It took ma friend Raphael a while to figure that out." Titus shook his head. "When she did, we were finally able to tell Duamutef the AI and Raphael the Human apart."

Jarvis' chest expanded with an intake of air. "Another hybrid! Like me!"

Titus' smile widened. Jarvis cringed as his hair was ruffled. "Yeh're partly right. Yeh were formed out of the merging with a protector bot, not an AI. Many sol-cycles ago, Zinkx was coming back from a recon mission into a Zaprex Way Station and found a child on the Plains of Blazing Fire. The kid was dyin'…"

Jarvis sat back in his chair. This was a story. He had to listen. Messenger stories were always incredibly important, that much he had learnt from Khwaja Denvy's long-winded tales.

"According ta Zinkx, the wee lass was so badly burnt there was barely anything left. He would tell us all that, as he knelt beside the dying child, the Zaprex canopic jar he had uncovered from the Way Station talked to him, told him to pour all the philepcon liquid over the child. So he did."

Jarvis blinked. "You're serious."

"Aye." Titus nodded. "That liquid was Duamutef and that child grew into Raphael." His master smiled fondly. "Who, like you, is a hybrid."

Jarvis shook his head, deflating slightly. "Hardly like me. She's the host of an AI! I'm just a protector bot."

Titus shrugged. "*Tah*, well, now yeh can see why we're contacting Duamutef."

"I cannot believe the House of Flames has a princess-class sky-ship."

"*Tah*, well…Raphael and Duamutef are actually a secret. And you will also remain one. When you get there. The House is not as accepting as yeh think it will be, laddie."

Jarvis nodded weakly. His master had reasons to think thus of his own people. After all, they had shunned him and his family simply for his being infected by a Twizel when they should have praised him for overcoming the parasite that had invaded him.

"How come you know so much about Duamutef?"

Titus scoffed. "Don' tell me yeh've never heard of the romantic tale of the Lady of the Tower and the Titan of Fire?"

"No…"

"No? No? Oh, yeh poor wee deprived laddie! Yeh've been robbed of the most wonderful fairy-tale since the Dawn of Time."

Jarvis gave his master a blank stare and sighed at his dramatic pose. "I much preferred my father's stories about the Ancient Starborn Paladins."

"Phff, romance stories have much more heart, more tragedy. They make yeh weep!"

"I promise I will tell your tale as a romance, Master." Jarvis threw him a smirk as he flicked a switch, and winced, hearing a painful whine burn through his skull. He clutched at his head and Titus' hand was on his shoulder instantly.

"Jarvis?"

"I think it's working." Jarvis peered through watering eyes. "The signal has been amplified." He glanced around the eerie room, trying to adapt his skin to the new, intense sensation of the brilliant song that was now playing through the crystals in the walls of the ancient vessel. They could only hope it would be sufficient to be picked up across the land and sky-sea: *Come to Utillia; come to safety.*

He settled back against the chair. It cushioned his weight naturally. Something about the whole environment made him feel entirely at ease, as though he had lived in the forlorn and forgotten world of the Zaprexes all his life.

"Master Titus, do you really think Khwaja Denvy is going to survive long enough to reach the House?" he murmured, just loud enough for the Hunter to hear. They had discussed the health of the old Kattamont many nights since crossing the border into Utillia, always making sure the other children were asleep, though Jarvis was sure that Ki'b knew Khwaja Denvy was dying.

Titus breathed out heavily. "I don' know. But a Messenger don' know the future, so we can only plan if we get the chance. T'be honest, laddie, the rate he be going, he won' live out the month."

Jarvis reached forward, gliding his fingers over the terminal and, without realizing he was doing it, he shut down the desk before him, pulling his crystal pendant free and looping it over his neck. His hand tightened around it. It had become his totem since the Time Master had led him to it. Khwaja Denvy believed the ancient Zaprex was guiding them always, and he had proof of that in his hands.

"Please, Time Master," he whispered, "don't let Khwaja Denvy die—"

Titus' sudden movement caught him off guard. It should not have; he was usually always alert to his surroundings and he knew that, later, his master was going to give him a tongue lashing. The Hunter grabbed him roughly by the shoulders and thrust him against a wall, pinning him down like he was a tiny pebble under a shoe.

"Ma...mast..er..." he choked out.

"Ki'rayh![4]" Titus' eyes gleamed, excitement causing his body to vibrate. Jarvis did not know whether he should relish the sight of

---

4   Ki'rayh (Key-rah) - High Class Twizels that have lived long enough to gain a personality beyond the Hive, and a True Name, which separates them from the Hive.

the young man's face morphing into a vicious snarl of delight, or be frightened by it. Then the words sank in, and his breath drained out.

His philepcon liquid froze in an ice grip around his hands, turning his skin blue as the slowly growing metal hull of his new changeling body hardened.

What was a High Class Twizel doing inside a buried Zaprex vessel? Jarvis reached for his colour-blade.

A trespasser. All trespassers must die.

He could hear and analyse their movements, pulses, and breathing long before they came into view: four Humans, one Kelib, and a Kattamont male who was much younger than Khwaja Denvy. He smelt their sweat and, in his heightened state of alert, with the philepcon liquid in his veins flooding his cybernetic exoskeleton, even the tiniest movements they made impacted against his scans. Jarvis' fingers tightened around the hilt of his sword, the metal layer of his protective hull hardening into thick armour as footsteps thudded past the doorway. He could not believe the stupidity of these men, entering a Zaprex ship so flippantly and without a care for the precious treasures within. They tore and hacked into it, chomping, biting, and ripping. Its song was no longer beautiful and melodious; it had turned into a wail of distress he could not tune out.

They followed the men, watching them patiently from the shadows. It took every ounce of his self-control not to leap out and kill the thugs for their painful disregard of Zaprex beauty. The only consolation he had was that his master was having just as much trouble holding himself back from the Ki'rayh that paraded itself around as an elderly Human man, shouting orders to the dismay of the young Kattamont male who looked fit to explode in an angry show of territorial air-gills and frilly fan-tail. Instead the Kattamont stalked off, tail irritably coiling back and forth, ignoring the laughter of the men he left behind as they dismantled a section of the central control room's platform. Jarvis hung above them in the awning of the ceiling, torn between dropping down, sword swinging, to kill all of them for touching that which was sacred, or slinking after the Kattamont youth. He reached out, tugging Titus' cloak twice, indicating his movement. His master nodded in reply and he carefully slid himself through the crystal panels, gracefully adjusting his weight as his hands, raw from the energy seeping from the crystals, clung desperately to the smooth surfaces. He trailed after the Kattamont, finding him bent over a terminal in the observatory deck. It was impressive that he had actually managed to turn it on, and it seemed he was reading the holographic projection screens, smiling with a look of contentment. His fur was no longer hackled, and his air-gills had flattened around his neck.

At least he was not tearing the ship apart to reach anything. He was showing respect, and that quelled the protector bot within him enough that he could process his thoughts logically again, instead of being overridden by the 'destroy' sequence running in the background of his programming.

Lowering himself from the ceiling, using his legs as ropes, Jarvis slid his blade against the throat of the Kattamont, feeling a great sense of delight when the air-gills spiked in sudden surprise.

"If you move, I will not hesitate to use this," he hissed.

"Been wondering when you would come out of the shadows," a considered tone replied.

Jarvis flicked his gaze in a quick scan of the room. "You came in here to speak to me?"

"You smell like the crystals. I was trying to figure out how one could be following us, I had hoped you might be a Zaprex."

Jarvis smirked. "No. Sorry. But I may be the closest you will ever get to one." He cocked his head to one side. Once he would have said that Kattamonts looked like the giant lions his father had taken out with sling and stone; now he was not so sure. Khwaja Denvy sure looked beast-like, but it seemed that just as Humans wore many faces, so did Kattamonts. Since entering Utillia, it was plain to see that Kattamonts were not beasts of burden. He was right now facing a Kattamont who was perhaps only a few sol-cycles older than he was, and was equally as calculating. Though his colour-sword was pressed against the neck of the young male, he had little doubt that they would end up in a well-matched fight. The black and silver coated feline did not carry the same heavy bulkiness of Khwaja Denvy. Instead he was slender, his limbs adapted for swift movement. Jarvis almost wished they could match blades, just to see what the result would be.

Carefully he lowered himself from the ceiling, landing on the terminal to stand atop it, so he would be taller than the Kattamont and able to rest his blade neatly against the male's neck. Beneath the odd mask contraption the Kattamont wore, his brow lifted ever so slightly. Jarvis wondered if he had caught the shine of his reflective skin, or the way his eyes glittered with an interior glow as his body whirred. He had begun to wear what Khwaja Denvy called the charismatic fairy grin, and he put it on for the Kattamont now, knowing it was as good as any off-putting sneer.

"Now, what are you doing here?" he queried.

The Kattamont's clicks and clacks were at least in Common Basic, easy enough to understand, but the fluidity of his accent was a little difficult; it was almost Imperial, from the cities—that was all he had to compare it with.

"I could ask you the same question."

"Ah, but I do not have a sword to my throat." Jarvis raised his brow. "I explore Zaprex ruins."

"Do you also rip them apart and make them cry?"

"I beg your pardon?"

"Your friends. They are ripping the star-glider apart. They cannot hear the pain they are causing it, but they are hurting the ship."

A low growl vibrated from the chest of the Kattamont. "They are Scavengers." His fur and feathers bristled in frustration. "I do not agree with their profession, but it is a way of life in Utillia. And they are not my friends."

"I am very glad we had this little conversation." Jarvis pressed lightly on his sword, inching forward. He increased the glow behind his eyes with a mental command. "Because if you had been trespassing upon my Creators' domain with ill intent, then your head would no longer be attached to your pretty furry body."

"Your Creators?" The Kattamont blinked rapidly. "Wait…what are you?"

Jarvis' attention shifted from the Kattamont, through the doorway and down the hall. The ship's sensor arrays were blaring at him long before he heard the chaotic shouts. The Kattamont did not act surprised when he lunged away, and he had the oddest impression the young feline already knew a fight had begun.

He paused briefly to yell back.

"If you want to live, stay here!"

His feet barely touched the floor as he ran down the corridor, heart pounding as the star-glider around him sang, calling him toward its central control room. He leapt over the overgrown crystals and into the fray of a fight. Half a dozen brawny men scattered as his master flayed amongst them, chasing after the Ki'rayh in Human form. Jarvis watched as Titus took off through a side door after the Dragon's fiend. His master's will must have snapped, and now all that was on the Hunter's mind was to kill and destroy the Twizel.

Most of the men had fled, but an arrow-bolt whistled past. Jarvis recoiled, looping through the air in a twist of gravity. He lashed out with his blade and fired blinding colour against a confused scavenger whose next shot from his crossbow fell wayward as the colours dazzled his vision. The weapon knocked against the ceiling. Jarvis swung a leg up, and cracked through the contraption the man held, whacking it aside as he thrust the man to the wall.

"You have trespassed," he snarled. The philepcon liquid of the protector bot within him gripped control of his limbs, and he had the distinct feeling the protector liked having a voice with which to speak through. "On my Creators' domain."

The man spluttered unintelligibly. Jarvis dodged something loud that burst from the man's hand, and the air filled with the smell of spicy heat. His eyes narrowed, locking onto a strange handheld metal object that was far smaller than a crossbow. Pictures flew across his optical screens, identifying a partial match to something similar: a pistol—this was a pistol, or a crude design of something the Zaprexes had encountered long ago. At least, it was in the archives of his mind.

"Drop that thing! If you wish to duel me, you will do it with a sword."

"I will kill you however I want, boy."

From behind, another man came barrelling down. Jarvis whipped around, blocking the force of the strike with an arm. The blade sheered through his skin, meeting his metal armour. His legs wanted to buckle under the weight of the huge man. Khwaja Denvy had always told him he needed to end a fight with a mortal in one or two strikes. They were not Twizels; they could be taken down and killed skilfully.

He gritted his teeth, surging his gravity-bubble outwards, thrusting it against the scavenger. Turning his sword in his grasp, he ducked as the second man also produced a pistol. The shot cracked near his ear and he cursed at the strange, alien thing. With a slash he cut through the man's groin, slicing the main artery, and knocking him back with a kick to the stomach. With a leap of gravity he parried with his blade, disorientating him in a blindfold of colour before scanning and striking cleanly through his neck. With the momentum of his fall, Jarvis thrust his leg forward, sending the man stumbling even as he clutched at his throat for the few moments left of his life.

Landing in a crouch, Jarvis wiped blood from his cheek. Then he stood, twirling his sword back into its usual position along his forearm. The sound deafened him, a split second before the flare of pain and the gushing of blood down his shirt. Jarvis choked on the shock, bending to slap his hand over the impact site that now looked like a crater in his chest filling with inky blue liquid and red blood. His sensors spun him in the direction of the first man he had encountered, leaning against the wall, holding his pistol in a trembling hand.

"*Jarkir!*" Jarvis swore. Grabbing his throwing dagger, he pitched it at the scavenger. It did not strike exactly where he had aimed, but it hit a kill spot, and the man slumped dead, his accursed weapon tumbled from his limp hand.

Jarvis resisted the urge to drop to his knees as he peeled back his hand. The wound was a gaping, bleeding hole in his chest and he stared at it in confusion. Nothing should be able to get through his armour plating. How had it penetrated his metal hull? Zaprex hulls could not be penetrated by a mere piece of metal. Jarvis staggered, swaying, and he clutched at the wound again, applying pressure. Already he could feel his systems beginning to flood the area; that which was still Human, still flesh, was going into shock; that which was cybernetic was assessing the damage and the readings flashed over his vision. He shook his head, trying to gain a clear path through the central control room. Master Titus carried a medical kit; if he could find him he could get some bandages.

Using his free hand, he dragged himself up the stairs, cursing each one until two strong paws grasped him under his arms and heaved him up as though he weighed naught. He looked up abruptly and faced the young Kattamont.

"You've been shot."

A sarcastic retort brimmed on the edges of his lips, but the concern in the Kattamont's crystal blue eyes triggered a bumbling tumble of confusion instead. "It…should not have been able to…get through my…hull."

"Mist-powered bullets. Made from the melted-down metal of Zaprex sky-ships. They will get through pretty much anything. Come on—I must get it out of you before it damages your internal systems."

Jarvis spluttered at the thought. What could melt Zaprex metal? The Kattamont was trying to get his shirt off him and he fought, scrambling away. He needed Master Titus. He did not need the help of some feline. The Kattamont reached out a paw towards him, mouth opening to speak something that he supposed was going to be reassuring in nature, but he never got the chance.

Three more men ducked through the crystal-blocked doorway, faces drenched in sweat. Jarvis staggered up into a fighting stance as they tore past, down the stairs, gathering their equipment. The Kattamont bellowed at them from the balcony.

"What's going on?"

"The Boss—he turned into something! We gotta get out. There's something trying to kill us."

The ship's pre-warning system flared in Jarvis' vision and he reacted despite his current lag. He leapt upon the Kattamont, bringing him down with a thrust of heavy gravity, ignoring how much his wounded chest screeched at him and the philepcon liquid that leaked onto the floor. The crystal in the doorway beside them shattered into shards and it took every ounce of his concentration to freeze them into place with his gravity-bubble as a half-transformed Twizel burst through.

"Torka!" the Kattamont snarled. "By the Rythrya Stones."

Jarvis wheezed out, gazing up with a mixture of disgust and misplaced wonder as the disjointed body of the old man tore itself into thin shreds, filling out into tentacles of thick, sludgy shadow with a mouth of acidic saliva. He had never before encountered a High Class Twizel, and, if the intense crackling pressure in the air was the result of being near one, then it was always going to be unpleasant. Talons of bone morphed out of the sludge and great wings expanded in a swirl. The mouth opened, releasing a high-pitched screech. It had no eyes he could see, but somehow Jarvis could feel it looking upon him and the Kattamont beneath him, and its anger was fuelled by a singular need—to kill.

"You sick old man!" The Kattamont howled, fan-tail expanding in rage. "You walked on my ship. You touched my queen! I swear to the Four[5], I will tear off your limbs!"

The Kattamont's words made no sense at all to Jarvis, but the creature's response was alarming. Jarvis gave the Kattamont a hard punch in the face.

"*Tarki,* moron! You've ticked it off."

"Let it come at me. I've wanted to kill the old fool for sol-cycles!"

Jarvis punched him again, infuriated that his blows were simply absorbed by the thick pelt. He swore as he was lifted up by two enormous paws and set down. A spear of pain went through his chest. He grappled for his sword to stand his ground as the Ki'rayh charged. The Kattamont crouched, preparing to bound as though to meet it halfway. Jarvis grabbed hold of the Kattamont's armour plates, dragging him back as the Twizel was struck in the side and rolled off the balcony, tumbling down amongst the confused and frightened scavenger men. Jarvis stumbled over to watch as Titus landed on the Ki'rayh with a shout, fists smashing into the monster's face.

"What in the burning-seas is that?" the Kattamont spluttered out, hanging onto the sides of the balcony's bent railings. He heaved himself over the edge, landing on the platform of the central control room. Jarvis panicked. Using his sword as a crutch, he hobbled down the stairs.

"No! No! Get out. Hurry!" He grabbed the Kattamont's arm, trying to drag him back.

"Wait. I can help—"

"Listen to me. My Master is not Human. He sometimes cannot see the difference between friend and foe. You have got to get out of here. That Twizel will either kill my Master or my Master will kill it." Jarvis seized up, proximity alarms flaring to the side of his vision. In front of him, the Kattamont made a movement with his wrist. Nothing touched him but he felt the backward momentum as he was hit by a thrust of wind that slammed him out of the path of the Twizel's tentacle. His body impacted a terminal. His mouth opened in a shout but his vision scattered into flecks. Everything around him dropped.

---

5   The Great Four Winds: North (Khamsin), South, East, West. Across Utillia the Kattamont Prides will tend to have affiliation with one, or all, of the Great Four. The Silvertide Pride was under the affiliation of the North until the casting out of Queen Zafiashid, when it is said that the blessing of Khamsin moved on with her.

Kı'в

CHAPTER THREE

They have called it the Thousand Sol-Cycle War.
I wonder what name it will be given a thousand sol-cycles from now,
dearest Sekhmet.
I grow weary, our children grow weary,
watching a world rip itself apart through war and hatred.
My mirrors reflect a light of a fading dawn age.
I feel so old, so tired, so alone.
I miss you.

Private Communications Link.
Utillian Time 6:09AM.
Signal: Good.
Upload: Completed.
Do you wish to send?

Denvy breathed heavily through his aching air-gills.

His body was decaying faster than he had anticipated. The trip over the Ovin-tu Mountains, crossing the path of the Three Little Kings, through thick snowfalls, vast forests, and rocky cliffs, had brought on a Humanlike illness to his now-mortal body. Titus believed something akin to pneumonia was attacking his respiratory system. He had never heard anything more ridiculous in his life. Kattamonts did not catch Human diseases.

He snorted at the preposterous thought and wearily shifted his weight against a wind-wrangled tree, one of many in the little cove they had found on the small island. A month prior they had crossed a pipeline between Pennadot and Utillia, used as a passageway for generations of traders. Since then they had hopped from island to island, with Titus growing increasingly concerned at the lack of land and the upsurge of the burning-sea. Not even the Hunter had been prepared for the wilderness of Utillia's deserts. It was like no other land.

Crossing the border had felt like a dream inside a hallucination. He was returning to the land of his birth, a land he had not wandered for many millennia—not since it had become a raging sea of sand. He blinked away ghosts of images that overlaid the horizon—looming coral reefs, dancing green and silver weeds shifting in the thick air currents. Shaking his head, he focused on the children playing in the lagoon of sparkling water.

Titus had found a small oasis island for their camp while he and Jarvis ventured further inland. Jarvis had adapted quickly to the different environment of Utillia, the air far denser than it was in Pennadot. The boy's body was changing on a cellular level. The other children, however, had struggled severely for the first few days, turning paler, movements slowing, and suffering awful headaches, their lungs unable to take in enough oxygen. It appeared the Zaprex turrets gleaming in the distance, still scattered over the ruined landscape, were not operating at full capacity, but the inadequate system was at least sufficient to aid in environmental adaptation—and eventually the children had recovered.

And now they were enjoying themselves, squealing and laughing as they played in the oasis pool, cooled by the shade of trees. The Sun roasted their skin, still scarred from the abuse they had endured at the hands of the Twizels over the course of their imprisonment. But they were free. The scars would forever remind them of the families they had lost, but they had forged new bonds, becoming a new family.

Clive kept a large shackle around one of his slender ankles; the Retenna boy claimed it was his trophy for surviving. He had taken up praying to the Sun again each morning, noon, and night, in honour of the Sun Monks who had been slaughtered when he had been taken captive. It was cruel, Denvy mused, that if only the lad's father, a travelling bard, had not left him at the temple to become a Monk... Well, everyone's threads travelled differently, he knew.

Sometimes, Denvy feared that Penny was the worst stung by their journey. The silver-tongued Obilb girl was bitter and frightened. She longed for the city of Tempath and the thick darkness of the mines where she felt she belonged. Maybe she truly did belong there, where silver ran deep into the earth.

"*Oie*! Khwaja Denvy, watch me do a boulder smash!"

Denvy lifted his weary head, brushing aside his air-gills. He caught sight of Clive at the last moment as the ruby-haired boy leapt into the water with a *whoop*, curling into a ball. Beside him, Ki'b released a pent-up howl of frustration as water splashed over her kit of herbs. The little Kelib girl leapt to her feet, ferocity shining in her eyes as Clive swam to the pools shore.

"Clive! Look what you did. You got water in my potions!"

He made a farting noise. "Your potions don't even work."

Penny clapped him over the head with a long stick. "You would be rolling around clutching your stomach still, Clive, 'cause of those berries you ate, if not for Ki'b's potions."

Clive swam away, making a show of gagging.

Ki'b shook her head, but slowly a smile came to her lips and the hands planted firmly on her hips returned to rest at her sides. She turned to face Denvy, her look far too mature for her age. "He is funny."

"I am glad you see his humour, dear one." Denvy winked.

Ki'b flicked back her short curls of hair. Since Titus had shaven it due to its matted state, it had grown considerably to cover her dainty, pointed ears. It was still not enough for her to hide her blushing cheeks behind, which often brought a grin to Jarvis' face whenever he teased her.

"*Tsk valai*, Khwaja Denvy." She used a high-class rebuke, having picked it up from one of his stories. "You sit back and rest! Let me rub my cream into your neck, so that nasty ring does not chafe anymore."

He chuckled, obeying her and settling back into the inlet of the tree roots, letting the wood take the weight of his aching muscles and heavy, lustreless fur. Ki'b scrambled her way up a root, perching herself neatly on his broad shoulder. With a joyful tune, she began to scoop up sweet-smelling cream to rub into the skin beneath the poisonous yoke around his neck. It would not bother her. To the tiny Kelib girl, it was nothing more than simple iron, but, to him, an ancient being from the Dawn Ages, the spell cast into the forging of it bound his immortality and his dreamathic mind.

This was not how he had expected to die—slowly, draining away, hour by hour, being eaten by a Human illness.

He snorted mucus. It was so ridiculous, it was almost hilarious. He would have laughed at the stupidity of it all, if he had any energy left to laugh with. He had to conserve all the energy he had for travelling, plodding one foot-paw before the other, in a body that had not been mortal in eons.

Denvy furrowed his brow. Could he even remember when he had last felt the real touch of the wind against his fur, or smelt the heat of the Sun through his nostrils? It had been so long since his foot-paws had burned with the agony of long travel. For centuries he had been an unyielding, solid, untouchable marble pillar that could not be beaten by time or elements. He had been the first program installed into Livila's mainframe by his Creators. There had been side-effects; he had endured them, accepted them.

A smile touched his lips and he closed his eyes. Maybe it was not so bad, dying as a mortal, feeling life in his veins again.

His ears twitched, catching the splashing of Clive and the annoyed shout the boy suddenly gave.

He turned toward the sound, grunting at the effort.

"*Oie! Oie!* Wha'cha think you're doing? You get away from my sistah!" Clive scrambled free of the pool, running for his pile of clothing, snatching up his dagger, ignoring his half-naked state and dripping wet limbs. The lad pinned the approaching figures with a furious glare.

Denvy's concentration was so slow and he cursed himself and whatever slug was currently eating his mind as his eyes finally focused on Penny, trembling against a tree as three Kelib men approached.

A foul stench hung in the air, and Denvy knew it was worse than what he could sense.

"Yuck." Ki'b covered her mouth. "They smell like rotting flesh."

Denvy ignored her unhelpful observation of her kin-people, however correct it was. The swagger in their walk was too confident as they approached the protective Clive, who was hissing like a kitten. They were like birds of prey, circling a dying carcass, and Clive was not the rotting corpse they had in mind. Denvy could feel them studying him. They would know a downed Kattamont when they saw one. He was an easy catch in his weakened state.

Denvy snarled, spreading his air-gills, despite the pain the terri-torial display caused his aching lungs. Ki'b's small hand gripped his leg. She would not be able to feel his agony, his dreamathic abilities were suppressed by the binding yoke, but she was observant.

The Alpha of the three Kelibs had sense enough to pause at the alarming colours of his gills, but the man's lips spread in a smirk nonetheless. Denvy narrowed his eyes. These were not Pennadotian Kelibs, who still had pride; these were members of a decayed society rotten to its core. The teeth that leered at him were foul and sharpened; between them a split tongue appeared. It might have hissed, if it could.

"What do you want?" Denvy gradually eased himself onto his foot-paws, careful not to make a sudden movement to set them off. Anything now would give them an excuse to kill Clive and Penny.

"*Oie!*" Clive barked. "Can you speak Common Basic, you ugly mutt-face!"

Denvy hissed at the boy. Clive ignored him, trying to inch closer to the frightened Penny. He was not doing a very good job at being stealthy by making himself so obvious, Denvy internally griped at the lad, wishing he had his dreamathic mind intact so he could mentally drag the boy back.

"*Balkr*, we want *yerk* pelt, kitty, kitty, and the little Human's night-skin." The tattooed Alpha made a vulgar sign at his throat.

Denvy's fur hackled. Poachers. He should have guessed from the putrid stench.

The stinging sound of drawing cutlasses rang in his ears and Denvy steadied himself, beginning a dark, deep growl. His body was weak, but it would last long enough to shield the children and give them a chance to escape. Ki'b inched herself into a fighting stance. He tapped his foot-paw twice, and she replied with three taps. She knew she had to run.

Two of the heavy Kelibs charged and Denvy swung his tail. The brittle spikes bent on impacting the chest of the nearest male, barely doing any damage to the rampaging poacher. He thrust the full weight of his shoulder against the man and twisted, throwing him high over his back. Agonizing pain speared his chest and he landed in a heap, clutching at his throat as he vomited blood.

Laughter erupted from the poachers, but nothing was more chilling than the feeling of cold steel against the nape of his neck.

Skinned alive. But then again maybe it was better to go down fighting than to die of a Human illness.

Clive shouted. Denvy snapped his head up. He wanted to hold out his arms, to order aloud that he not intervene, that he run to the girls, but it was too late. Clive was in motion. He leapt upon the Kelib, driving his small dagger into the flesh of a shoulder.

"Get away from Khwaja, you monster!"

Denvy struck out with his tail, throwing the Kelib off balance. The poacher staggered back and Clive howled as he slashed viciously at the man's throat. It was scarcely enough to scratch the surface of the thick hide. The Kelib wrenched Clive aside, holding him out with a bloodied hand.

Clive spat into his face before the air was choked from him. Denvy staggered towards him, yelping as a blow sent him elbows first into the soft dirt. The girls had made it around the pool, but Penny was screaming for Clive. Denvy clawed the grass, bellowing as a sword sliced down his spine. He had failed his cubs. He was nothing without his immortality; he may as well have been dead to them.

Clive's head dropped back, his limbs slackening. No longer could Denvy feel pain. The boy's life was draining away before him. The leering Kelib holding him pulled out a knife and made a movement to scalp his precious fiery hair.

Denvy choked on the blood in his throat, speaking a desperate spell, despite the knowledge it would be useless with the yoke binding him. The words hung comfortingly on his tongue. At least he had tried.

An arrow speared through the skull of the Kelib, the bone bursting with the speed and enormity of the weapon that was now buried in the flesh of a nearby tree. The fletching feathers were not of a bird; they were the fins of a male Kattamont's mating gills.

"Release the cub, Kelib scum, or I will tear you limb from limb," a refined female voice spoke maliciously.

Denvy blinked away tears, turning his head weakly. He peered through his air-gills. Whether from blood-loss or pain, or simply his addled mind tricking him, what he saw was surely not real—in a wheelchair, a young Kattamont sat proudly, holding a bow of twisted crystals. A brilliant pink fan-tail rattled in provocation. She wore a merciless grin, directed at the Kelib men.

Denvy had not thought it possible for a Kelib male to look frightened, and yet the ghastly tattooed face of the Alpha had drained of blood. Though he himself had not recognized the voice that had shrilled out, nor the Kattamont sitting territorially in the wheelchair, the Kelibs certainly did, and the arrow that had slain so easily was no mere threat. She meant to kill again.

The Alpha's remaining brother shouted a bull's roar, tearing across the oasis in the direction of the girls. Denvy stooped for the blade dropped by the slain Kelib, using it as a crutch to drag his trembling body upright. The yoke felt like a powerful counterforce; he was unable to reach his cubs. Ki'b stood her ground, rooted like a tree as she stared down the raging Kelib male. Behind her, Penny had curled into a ball.

Denvy cringed as the Kelib lunged. From the branches of the trees above, a blur of silver, black, and vivid iridescence shot down, hurtling into the charging Kelib, smashing him into the ground with a crack. It was a Kattamont queen, with a pelt as rich as charcoal. Her jaw closed around the neck of the poacher, spraying blood. The Kelib struggled, smashing fists and knees into the female, yet her pelt absorbed every hit. Suddenly the queen reared up and threw the flailing Kelib into the air. She shouted and Denvy watched as another arrow sailed past. The massive shaft howled as it was released, carving the body in half.

She turned as blood rained down around her, the frenzy of the hunt wild in her eyes as she focused on the Alpha pinning Denvy to the ground. The blade at his throat tightened against the muscle and he dared not breathe out. Her tail whiplashed back and forth as she began to stalk forward, a feral grin spreading over her bloodied lips. Her fan-tail burst with a rocket of dazzling colour and she bounded in a surge of speed. The blade at Denvy's throat cleaved, but he only heard the roar and felt a heavy weight leave him as the queen struck the Kelib and dragged him down. The magnificent shadowy female rolled before her tail's feathers pulled back to reveal blades. With a crack and pop she hewed head from shoulders. The Alpha's scream died abruptly. The queen held the head up, smirking.

"Poachers. Forever the scourge of our seas."

Denvy turned and emptied the contents of his stomach, coughing and spluttering blood as it drained from his lungs. He put a paw to his throat, wondering if the Alpha had managed to cut through. Was he bleeding out? Was he dead? How long did it take to die? For *Hazanin's* sake, was it supposed to be this laborious?

"Mother!" He heard the shout and the nearby sound of gears clanking together. Wheels entered his blurry vision. "It is a prince."

A prince? He had not heard himself called the title of a male Kattamont in centuries. He wanted to laugh. The word made him sound young and valiant. He snorted. He had been around Humans far too long.

"Don't you go near Khwaja Denvy!" Ki'b made her presence known. Denvy felt her tight hands grab him, her small fingers seeking the bleeding wound and ruthlessly pinching the skin closed. "You horrible monsters!"

She had become a very feisty little girl, a true testament to her ancestor barbarian queens. His ears twitched as he heard a clattering of stones against wheels grinding over the ground and the wheel-chair stopped nearby. Strangely it was the diplomatic voice of the wheelchair-bound neutral that purred out, rather than the queen's.

"Please. We mean you no harm. If you let me, I may be able to help him. But I need to get him back to our sand-ship."

"You don't understand." Ki'b's tears splashed over his nose. "He can't be healed. He doesn't heal! His wounds don't…they don't stop. You can't heal someone who is cursed to die."

How it hurt to hear the pain in Ki'b's voice. He did not wish it upon her, the agony he was causing her through her love for him.

"Ah, by the Winds! Curses? Such nonsense! We shall see about this. Come, you little whelps, back to the sand-ship."

He was grabbed roughly under the arms and dragged upright. The queen lifted him and slung him over her back. "*Tah*, like I would leave a prince this old to die such a pathetic death with females wailing all over him. Nixlye, leave an arrow to mark our kill. Fetch the unconscious little prince-whelp while you're at it. We shall see about breaking nonsense curses. You, little Kelib princess, hurry up! We do not have all day."

Denvy heard Ki'b shout something in Common Basic that sounded like one of Titus' overly-flamboyant Trench profanities, but he was too surprised by the lack of pain in his lower extremities. Then he realized he was, in actual fact, being carried by the queen. Not since he was a cub could he recall being carried—maybe lugged was a better word, but, even so, for the queen to be able to bear his weight was unbelievably impressive.

He must have said so. He was not entirely sure how the words escaped his mouth, since his lips were numb and his head ached. Everything was fuzzy.

She snorted in offense. "I have lifted crates heavier than you, prince. You are nothing but shaggy fur and bones. It is going to be a long time before you are fit for anything but looking after cubs."

He was about to tell her he was fine with looking after cubs; he had been doing it for centuries. But somewhere between his growl and her laughter, he lost consciousness.

SEMYUERU

CHAPTER FOUR

You speak of missing me when I am but a thought away.
You are surrounded by our children, who still love you.
The Dragon has not yet taken from us our Dynasty.
He has stolen our ability to give life, but
he has not taken our will to live.
You will succeed in your task, Nefertem.
I do not doubt you, so do not doubt yourself.
I look down from above and I see the work you and our children do.
I am proud.
Save Livila.
Fight.
We are Zaprexes.

We save worlds, or we die trying.

NORTHERN TOWER – PRIVATE COMMUNICATION LINKAGE –
01010011 01100101 01101011 01101000 01101101 01100101 01110100

Jarvis was sure he was back in the box that had imprisoned him. The Human part of him was frightened; it feared the enveloping darkness groping at his limbs and tugging at his skin. But the protector bot whispered reassurance.

He had no reason to fear. The darkness meant him no harm. The longer he floated, drifting in the rhythm of a gentle river, the clearer the new world became and gradually he was immersed in scatterings of tiny lights. It was as though he was swimming in the night sky-sea, swirling and dancing with the stars themselves. Jarvis stared at his skin, admiring its new texture, covered in the same pattern of stars as the network surrounding him. Each time he stepped he left behind an open glowing footprint and through that hole he was sure he could see Pennadot, but he had never seen Pennadot from far above before. Maybe he was in the sky-sea; he had become a star. Maybe he was dead and he was travelling to the Sun.

"No, you are not dead, my precious little body. This is the network of the world, the Data-Stream, or, as you mortal flesh-bags call it, the Secondary Realm. Welcome, Jarvis of the Plains People, to the greatest machine the Zaprexes built—otherwise known as my prison."

Jarvis froze. The sense of beauty and tranquillity of his surrounds was broken. Something immense was behind him, choking him with its enormous existence, wrapping around him like a cloak with fingers. His head turned, eyes settling upon a flame-haired figure standing on a red-lit circle, with corresponding chain patterns across pale, freckled skin. It was a boy, younger than he was, perhaps about Clive's age. But no boy he knew, not even annoying, bothersome Clive, had ever looked so cruel. He was reminded of a spider, crawling towards a helpless fly tangled in its web.

Jarvis was the fly.

He gasped, as suddenly the boy was inside his own circle, and the red hue was all around him, burning away his blue colours.

"Your body is not my style. Not really what I was going for—a bit mundane. But I suppose I will grow to like it." He leered. "Funny that: growing into something. Me, trying to fit into you. I am the size of a planet. I don't think it will work, no matter what my minions tell me."

Jarvis flinched as a hand touched his chin. The skin was hot. A sharp pain struck him in the skull and he held his head as light dazzled his eyes. It was unbearable, worse than when he had felt the protector in the Zaprex Way Station die in front of him. Claws dragged into his skull, trying to tear through the layer of the protector's program, and it was fighting back, screeching at him to regain control and win against the boy laughing at them. How could he fight something that was in his head?

"Dragon!"

Jarvis jerked back. He had been so transfixed by the bottomless pits of eyes void of everything, unable to move and speak, terrified by the hopelessness that had gripped him. He had not moved, though he had believed he had.

The high-pitched screech that rang out was like a blaze through the starry realm, sending a pulse into the galaxy. Everything swelled into rivers, forming long arms that unfolded from a singular point and standing in the centre of the spirals was an infuriated Zaprex holding up a finger.

The protector that shared his body confirmed that it was indeed a Creator and his relief was immeasurable. If only the sweet face was not set in such rage, it would have been beautiful.

"Back away from the protector bot," the Zaprex snarled, "or I will unleash upon you everything I know if you come even one grid-step closer."

Jarvis gasped. The movement was involuntary; he floundered away from the smirking boy standing behind him, splashing into the silver spiral. He dashed across its surface, kicking up starry codes as he moved.

"It is all right. Do not panic. He cannot hurt you with me here. Follow the sound of my voice; come to my grid-polygon."

Jarvis ran. It felt as though he ran for miles, when it may have been mere metres, but there did not seem to be such a thing as distance in this eerie world. Eventually he found himself surrounded by the swelling of stars, coating him protectively.

The Dragon was still there, just beyond him, leering with empty eye sockets and a wide, toothy grin that chilled him to the core. A touch stirred him and he looked down at the beautiful fairy. It was not the Time Master, who had led him to the Zaprex Way Station. The Time Master had an air of great age; this Zaprex was tiny and he guessed it was young.

It was a child.

The Dragon waded closer to them, making the hair of the Zaprex behind him stand on end in a static charge. It hissed in irritation.

"Hello, little Key! How lovely of you to join us—"

"Silence! I know what you are trying to do and it is not going to work. If you attempt to take over this protector bot again, you will not get a chance to enjoy having a body. When we meet face to face, I will tear it apart!"

The Dragon's hands fisted and Jarvis cringed as the black world rippled. He watched in horror as the boy's image wavered. But the Zaprex waved a hand and stabilised the distortions.

"It is strange, little Key, how different you are to your beloved people. It took them centuries to decide on violence, and, even then, it backfired on them."

"Do not think that you will bother me with tales of my people, Dragon. I am beyond that. You cannot taunt me. Now you will either remove yourself from my presence, or I will make you." The Zaprex levelled the Dragon with a glare.

"You think you can fight me? Not even the combined forces of your entire Empire could defeat me!"

"No. But I will send out a distress signal that will run an anti-virus in this area, and I am sure you do not want that, do you? They are a bit like jailers to you, I imagine…heh?"

The Dragon hissed, spitting liquid as it turned sharply. "You are nothing like Hazanin. Hazanin was a crazy lunatic, far easier to manipulate—"

"Insult my Positive Parent again," the Zaprex snarled, stepping closer, yellow eyes glazing into a red film," and I will show you just how much like Hazanin I am."

"Such ferocity." The Dragon bent forward. "Do you get that from your Human guardian, or from the Kelib? Oh, which one will I kill first when I am free? Maybe…the Human—"

Jarvis flinched as the Zaprex moved. It was like a flash, so fast the light could not keep pace with the imp. It appeared before the Dragon and lashed out, the Dragon stumbled back with a shout. The surface beneath them scattered with symbols as the Zaprex swung out a leg, smashing it into the Dragon's waist and striking him against the floor. Around them alarms flared. Jarvis curled into a ball as the blackness turned red, as red as the eyes of the small Zaprex. The Dragon choked, hands flayed out in a protective shield.

"You cannot harm me!" the Dragon rasped. "It is against the mandate of your people to kill. You cannot kill me! You cannot kill; you value life too much. If you hurt me, you will destroy the very memory of your race. You...do not want to do that...do you...little Key?"

The Zaprex lifted its foot. "My people are already dead, Dragon. I am the last one, therefore I think I can decide what I want to do to honour them. Now be a good little worm and slither off to your hole."

In a burst the Dragon scattered into flecks, only his haunting voice remaining.

"We will meet again, little Key, and you will burn, just as your people did!"

The Zaprex shook itself and Jarvis watched as remains of the Dragon's clinging flakes rippled off the imp. "If I burn, it will be because I choose to burn, Dragon," it muttered.

Jarvis would have held his breath but he was sure he did not actually have breath to hold in this realm of energy. His mind could not comprehend that he was within another plane of existence—the place of Elementals and spirits. His family—was his family here? His eyes darted toward a bright star in the distance, the giggling he could hear. It might have been Ki'b, or even his sister.

The Key snatched his wrist.

"Do not follow the will-o'-the-wisp; we only lead you astray."

"What are they?" He looked down at the pixie, and the flowing heads of the antennae daintily bobbing free from the centre of its head. The Zaprex smiled sadly.

"They are other Zaprexes. Lost programs. There was a great calamity; I do not know what it was, but it was a terrible disaster that broke the cycle of my people's existence, a cycle that I must begin again. Come—you are part Human; you will want to escape into the bliss of Eternity. I need to get you back to your terminal." It tugged his hand gently and he stumbled after the floating Zaprex. "This way."

The trails of the galaxy followed them, as though they were connected to the fairy's movements, though what it represented he could not fathom, and the protector within him had no knowledge of the Key to feed into his mind. It appeared as though the tiny imp was in deep thought, muttering to itself, something about a 'Gifu and Positive Parent'. It was beginning to look despairingly concerned, the grip on his wrist growing tighter.

"Are you all right?" Jarvis offered softly.

The Zaprex squeaked and turned sharply. It stared at him with bright eyes, unblinking under the curls of its soft raven hair. Suddenly it beamed a huge smile and twirled away from him in a dance.

"I am fine," it chirped.

"I...ah..." Jarvis rubbed his nose, hearing a giggle from the Zaprex. "I should thank you for saving me."

A nonchalant shrug returned his thanks. "It would appear you called me here, so I had to come."

Jarvis frowned. "I called you?" The signal—was it possible that the signal he had sent out through *Bez-at:_Who_Lingers_by_Water* had already been heard, and by a Zaprex? Of all the possible recipients he supposed it would be a Zaprex who would have picked it up first. "The signal I sent out—you heard it?"

"So you did send the song?" The Zaprex settled on its heels. "The frequency you used is set to a particular molecule; it would resonate with only me and those who are related to me. How you received this information is beyond my comprehension right now. It is rather... unpleasant...and I request that you reduce the volume or turn it off. I doubt it is having a nice effect on Gifu. Poor Gifu. His brain must be all mushy by now."

Jarvis frowned. Surely he was not addressing *the* Duamutef, Lady of the Tower, Titus had told him about? That was the only other possible Zaprex connection that he knew anything about.

"I am sorry. I am rather," he rubbed his hands together, "new at working Zaprex technology."

"I presumed this was the case when I saw you were a hybrid. Like I said," the Zaprex smiled, waving a hand about dismissively, "tone it down or turn it off. Actually...why are you sending out a song, anyway?"

Jarvis jogged to keep up with the dancing pixie who had skipped ahead of him. Whatever was he supposed to say to it? Was it all right to tell a Zaprex what was going on? Master Titus would approve, would he not?

"We're Messengers, you see, and my Master received a message from Commander Zinkx about the eruption of Coltarian come the Midsummer Solstice. My Master was sure that if we used this song to get a signal out, someone at the House of Flames would pick up the message I coded into it."

The Zaprex advanced on him, causing him to skid to a halt. "What is your designated code?"

Jarvis frowned. Code? The protector bot within him threw up a few symbols, and he relaxed. He almost chuckled. "You...ah...mean my name? It's Jarvis, son of Jerark, of the Plains People. I was captured by Twizels but we escaped some months ago, along with some other children. We were being taken to Utillia, though we are not sure why. My Master saved us."

"My designated code is Semyueru," the Zaprex touched its chest, "but you are welcome to call me Sam. It is what my protectors call me."

"Sam." Jarvis smiled, letting the word pop out of his lips. It was so very simple.

"I actually like Sami." The Zaprex tipped its head to one side, a tinge of blue touching its cheeks. "My newest companion has begun to refer to me by that name. I think it is a form of affection, though I am not sure. My processing of such things is still in progress. Well, Jarvis of the Plains People, how did you become a hybrid?"

"Oh," Jarvis laughed. "I suppose I followed a will-o'-the-wisp into a Zaprex Way Station. The Time Master, actually, but I didn't know at the time who I was following. I was attacked by a machine inside when I found this crystal—"

Tugging open the rim of his silver suit, Jarvis relaxed at the sight of the precious triangular prism still attached to the chain around his neck. He pulled it out, revealing it to Sam. The Zaprex had gone entirely slack, but by the vibrating buzz in the air, he had the feeling the imp was suppressing a vast amount of energy.

"My Master, thankfully, came and dealt with the machine but not before I was contaminated by its philepcon liquid."

He heard Sam breathe in sharply. The Zaprex twirled a hand in the air, bringing up an information screen suspended in the air, flicking through pages of scrolling symbols. The smile that had formed over the imp's face began to dissolve and its antennae flopped.

"I…should warn you…the area where you are currently is going to destabilize soon." Sam glanced up.

"It is?"

"Yes. Have you not been picking up the warning signal?"

"You mean the weird blinking thing on the side of my vision." Jarvis tapped his temple. He had not thought anything of it. It had been around for days, almost since they had entered Utillia. He had believed it a malfunction in his optical lenses.

"Yes, that." Sam sighed heavily.

"Oh, that's what it's for?"

"Yes, you need to get out of here and leave wherever you are now." The Zaprex shoved him roughly.

Jarvis stumbled. "Can you come with me?"

"No. The defragmentation station in your ship is defective, but, even so, I would not abandon Gifu and Gibo. And there is no defragmentation machine on my side either. This is problematic. Your body is also damaged, but you are recovering. Nothing vital was hit. Fortunately the lung that was injured has already begun its transformation. I am impressed, Jarvis; you absorbed the philepcon liquid of a protector class robot and survived. According to the user-manual in my hard-drive, if they do contaminate a carbon creature, they usually reject the host…as per protocol. Maybe it liked you." Sam drew up another information screen, surrounding them both in a scattering of holographic displays. Jarvis spun around. It was the central control room he had been in. He gasped. Master Titus. He could see the Hunter bending over a body—it was his body.

"So, I really am a Changeling?" Jarvis murmured.

The Zaprex shifted, studying him before laughing suddenly. Jarvis frowned at the bubbling giggle.

"That was the correct term for a hybrid that was not born from a Zaprex-Human union, yes. Once…long ago. I suppose you will be the first in a very long time. Here—this is your terminal. You must log out."

"Thank you." Jarvis inclined his head. "It had been an honour to meet you."

"The honour has been mine, Jarvis of the Plains People: you have my last Map piece." The Zaprex pointed to the crystal prism around his neck. Jarvis wrapped his fingers around it. Sam giggled, tugging out a necklace of its own, holding it forth. Jarvis' eyes widened at the sight of three triangles, set together in a prism. Sam held it elegantly in the palm of its hand, causing the crystals to shimmer to life, activating at a silent command. Jarvis squeezed his own precious crystal protectively.

"This is…this is yours?"

"I need it for my function to save the world."

"You do? Can you take it now?"

Sam shook his head. "Without a defragmentation station, no, matter cannot pass through the Data-Stream. If the Time Master led you to it, then this is part of a bigger painting that you and I cannot see. Maybe this is what you carbon creatures call luck…fate…I do not know. If you are willing to take the task upon yourself…" Sam tilted its head to one side. "Jarvis, I must ask you to wait for me at the House of Flames. I will come for my Map piece and you must guard it."

Jarvis inclined his head, bowing low. "It is a task worthy of someone who is carrying the blood of a fairy-machine. Khwaja Denvy will be very glad to know that I can do this for you, little Key."

The fairy touched his forehead and he looked up. Its face was a mixture of confusion and amusement, and he wondered if he had said the right words. The protector bot within him hummed that he had, but maybe it was the little Key who truly did not know how to act before him. Sam scratched behind an ear, motioning to a bright glowing screen.

"Go, and may the Sun guide your path," it whispered. "And, ah, try not to log into the Data-Stream again. Ever. Best not tempt the Dragon to eat you…"

"I won't. I assure you of that."

He sucked in a deep breath, unwilling to leave the presence of the fairy and the harmonic song it radiated. Jarvis squeezed shut his eyes. Truly he could have remained by the Key's side forever, lost in its song, but he focused on Ki'b's face, her happy smile, and her bright laughter; it was as sweet as any Zaprex's. Slowly he stretched out his hand. His fingers brushed the screen. Folding white light streamed around him, and he was pulled away with a tight tug. The rough sensation of being shoved back into the tight confines of his body was painful, and a bolt of electricity jolted him upright with a loud shout. Jarvis fumbled around, clutching at his burning chest, gasping for air.

The bullet was still wedged in his side, the wound beginning to sizzle and crackle. He felt over it for the hole. At least the bleeding had stopped. His philepcon liquid had dealt with the damage to the hull, but something had indeed been struck, and it was not yet connected to his cybernetics, so he could not figure out what it was.

A twittering laugh echoed off to the side of his ear and he cocked his head, frowning in confusion. He looked around the control decks, finding only himself and the wreckage of the fight. Jarvis tapped his ear, before giving his head a whack. If Sam was still in the mainframe, maybe it was laughing at him through the terminal. He pouted and glared at the floating glass desk. This was just what he needed, a fairy laughing at him for his stupidity at getting shot and almost consumed by their great enemy.

Another giggle. This time it faded away, leaving his philepcon liquid aching tightly against his bones. The fairy was gone and he was alone.

"Jarvis! Oh, yeh sweet little laddie!"

Well—not entirely alone.

The reason he had been ruthlessly cast into the strange world of the Secondary Realm became clear as Titus' heavy body smothered him. There had been a ghastly fight between the scavengers, the Twizel, and his master. Had his master won? Surely he had if he was now hugging him. Titus did not seem bothered that his cloak was steeped in Twizel and Human remains, nor that he smelt horrendously foul. He dragged him into a crushing embrace, stuffing his face into his chest. Jarvis choked back a gag.

"Master…I…my chest. I am wounded."

"I thought yeh were dead! Yeh friggen heart had stopped. Don' yeh ever do that ta me again, yeh little scallywag."

His master pulled away and studied him with an unimpressed scowl. "We need ta patch yeh up."

"I am fine, sir, really." He might have been swaying on his feet a bit, but he could stand. "Did you get the Ki'rayh?"

He looked around the room and noted the butchered bodies. It was a scene he was glad Ki'b and Penny were not witness to. Surely his master had not done all this damage. He knew the man could be ruthless to his foes, but they were mainly Twizels who copped his merciless wrath, not mortal men.

"Ah, no, it got away." Titus sank back and Jarvis felt the need to hyperventilate as the freckled features of his master vanished, replaced with the skeleton. "I never had one get away before," the Hunter snarled. "This one was different, Sonny Jon. Yeh would not have believed it! Something was not right. This is gonna come back and bite me in the *totu*, I know it is!"

Titus grabbed Jarvis' arm with a bony hand. "We got another problem."

Jarvis squeaked as he was hauled through the control room and dumped in front of the young Kattamont male who had thrust him out of harm's way and into the terminal. Jarvis felt his chest, grateful that his new metal skeleton could absorb a rough landing, because whatever had thrown him had done it with almighty force. With his hull already breached by the bullet, he shuddered at the thought of what could have happened had the wound ruptured more than it already had.

"It was him?" Jarvis whispered at the slumped-over feline. "He did this?" He stared around at the ruins of the CCR, and the bodies that may as well have been shredded. His chest constricted, but if the agonizing torture and deaths of his family had done one thing it had at least desensitised him to everything else he had seen since that fateful day.

"Oh, yah." Titus thumped down his heavy stone-giant sword, leaning on it casually. "I would like yeh ta meet Aaldryn Silvertide— an archaeologist who explores Zaprex ruins to learn about ancient Utillia."

"Did you knock him out?" Jarvis turned sharply, glaring in accusation at the skeleton.

"Nope. Even if I wanted, I wouldn't be able ta. He's got a bit of an advantage, this fella—havin' a god in his head."

Jarvis back away suddenly.

"A…god!" he spluttered out. He had put his sword to the throat of a god? What type of god? One of the Kelibs' forest-gods? Ki'b would flay him alive if he had done that!

"Oh, well, they like ta think that's what they be." His master chuckled. "Nah. They're just Elementals with a bit more clout than their offspring." Titus clicked his bony fingers. "Here we all thought the Titan of Fire was the only one to survive the culling of the Olympians. Come on, yeh wind-bag, stop pretending to be snoring! I know yeh're in there. I can feel the residual energy yeh're radiating. I'm an Elemental, too. Don' try ta hide from me."

Aaldryn's head lifted, though limply, like a straw doll, his eyes glazed. His lips moved without there being any sign of consciousness within what should have been a vibrant and powerful figure.

"Prometheus lives?"

Fold, over fold, Titus' skin returned as though painting his skull. A kind smile formed over the man's features. It made his freckled cheeks light up handsomely. "Yes, yeh big horn-blower, he does. Yeh're not alone."

"My children have not spoken of this to me, and my children fly to all corners of the Northlands."

"Coltarian has its own weather system. Possibly they can't get in there."

The Kattamont's chest inflated. "True."

Titus spread his hands. "So, trust me when I say Prometheus lives. Yeh know I'm telling yeh the truth, 'cause yeh can feel it in my bones." He touched his chest, giving it a pat of assurance. "Prometheus is goin' to be shooting fire to learn yeh be lazing about just over the border."

"I am not lazing about!" The wind-god stood suddenly. Jarvis stumbled back at the sight of the Kattamont's limp body swinging upright. "I protect this mortal's life, and the lives of those around him. It is my repentance, thus I shall forever remain bound to mortal flesh! And this land is decaying. There is a rot within it that I and my children have been trying to repel for centuries. I will never again ascend to the realm of Olympus."

Jarvis frowned. "What is Olympus?"

"It be what the Elementals call the Secondary Realm." Titus heaved his sword over his shoulder. "Wind-god—"

"Khamsin. My name, little Shadow, is Khamsin."

"*Tah, tah*, whatever." Titus shrugged. "I think Prometheus' chains are being broken. The Obelisks are falling one by one. Coltarian is in danger of erupting. Any idea who could be doing that? Yeh're old, right? Older than the hills, and I bet yer memory is better than old man Denvy's."

Khamsin eyed Titus thoughtfully.

"How do you know so much about what I am?"

"The Titan of Fire used ta rock me to sleep when I was a wee little laddie. I am the last in a large family, and was not welcomed by my brothers, so yeh could say, I was raised by the Thyrrhos. Got the hair for it, yeh know."

Khamsin snorted. "Typical of Prometheus. His love of mortal kind has been the doom of us all."

"Hey—" Jarvis narrowed his eyes. "You just said that you're looking after Aaldryn and those around him. Isn't that the same thing?"

"Do not speak of things you know nothing of, Changeling. You have much to learn." The Kattamont's body stood limply. "Prometheus once regulated the ebb and flow of kinetic energy throughout the planet's sectors. It may be possible, by eradicating my siblings' system, one could gain control of it. You would need to seize control of Icarus, though. And the Towers as well."

"Icarus?" Titus turned to the wind-god in confusion. "Who is Icarus?"

"I do not know what it is called now, but it was one of the Cities of Gold. This cub that contains me is part of a crew who searches for their wonders."

"I don' like the sound of this." Titus frowned and Jarvis blew out as his master began to undo his medical supplies, inching towards him as though he was unsuspecting prey. "The Dragon really is up to something. We gotta get back to Coltarian sooner rather than later."

"Before it blows up? Yes." Jarvis sniped back.

"That would be preferable." Titus' glance was disproving. Any other smart comments would likely result in a far more disgruntled master. It was time to play it safe.

Jarvis looked at the Kattamont. "Ah, where is Aaldryn? That is his name, right?"

"He thought he killed you. He is unconscious. He rather liked you."

"So you killed all these men?"

Khamsin shrugged. "They were just men."

Jarvis frowned. He wondered if Aaldryn felt the same, or if this was only the powerful elemental god speaking.

"By the way," Titus began unrolling bandages from his kit, kneeling beside him and cutting through his shirt with a knife, "what happened to yeh, Little Weasel? Yeh had no heartbeat for a long time, laddie."

Jarvis winced as Titus inspected the bullet wound, spraying it with alcohol from his flask. His hull sizzled. It was about as happy as he was at the treatment.

"The bullet is still in there, sir."

"Aye, but I don' wanna take it out without my full medical kit. I got a feelin' yer philepcon liquid is stopping the pain right now, but a possible overload of your systems will hit yeh soon. Yeh aren't quite a full hybrid yet, laddie. I'll carry yeh on my back."

Jarvis pouted. That would look so heroic when he returned to Ki'b. She was going to have a fit at him for this and would never again let him out of her sight. His chest inflated as he remembered—Sam had given him a task and, no matter what, he had to complete it.

"Jarvis!"

Titus' hand scrubbed through his hair. "Laddie, wake up."

"Sor…ry…sir…"

"All right, I think yeh've lost too much philepcon liquid. Yeh're spazzing out. Khamsin, we need a way outta here. How did yeh and the scavengers get in?"

"Wait! Master!" Jarvis held out his hand, stalling the hunter before he could gather him into his arms. "Please. You need to hear this. When I hit the terminal, I connected with the Secondary Realm and I met the Key! That signal I set out, it hurt the Key. I need to tone it down."

Titus held up his hands in frustration. "What? But that code should only be linked to Duamutef."

Jarvis got to his feet and staggered up the stairs, towards the terminals.

"Well, it isn't, sir. The Key picked it up too. And…" Jarvis stopped fiddling with the controls and turned to beam at Titus. "It gave me a task!" If his chest had not been aching so much, it might have swelled with pride.

"A task?"

"Aye, sir! I must take this," Jarvis held up the dangling sliver of crystal, "to the House of Flames. It isn't just any old thing. The Time Master led me to it. It's special. The Key needs it."

Titus' looked up at the ceiling. "Oh, for the love of mah wife, I knew the Time Master was in on this!"

Khamsin's voice bellowed from beyond them. "The Time Master is moving again? Does this mean the nest of the beast has begun to stir?"

"The Dragon is rising, Khamsin." Titus looked across at the young Kattamont and skewered the elemental god with a stare that made Jarvis shrink back. "Yeh're gonna have ta choose which side yeh're on."

As if he were moving a show puppet, like those the bards used in the market squares, Khamsin moved Aaldryn's limp body, viciously confronting Titus' dark aura with one just as engulfing. "The wind does not choose a side. The wind is free. Let us be clear on that."

Jarvis squeaked as Titus lifted him and threw him over his shoulder. "The wind also runs away! I hope, Khamsin, that this time we can rely upon yeh *not* ta flee from the field of battle when we most need the wind. Come on, let's get back. Khwaja Denvy is likely to be worried by now and this tyke needs mending."

"Not before I fix the signal!" Jarvis waved his arms about.

"*Tah*, fine, fine!" Titus relented, setting him down.

Jarvis smiled weakly. His master looked haggard from the battle, but his gaze was a worried one, and he knew the Hunter was concerned entirely for his welfare. His hair was ruffled fondly. It was nice to be worried about.

PRINCESS NIXLYE OF THE MISFIT PRIDE

CHAPTER FIVE

In the depths of my despair, your words bring light and hope.
I feel so often the weight of the burden Ra gave me.
To bind together the Northlands, to save Livila…
Sekhmet, my dearest, I am afraid, our Dynasty will die doing so.
And, yet,
Whenever your words whisper through the crackling com-link,
I recall…
Yes, the Dragon took our life-giving, but he never took my creations.
They will live on.
Our song
Will sing until the Key begins a new symphony.

Private Communications Link.
Utillian Time 18:03PM.
Signal: Strong.
Upload: Completed.
Do you wish to send?
Yes. Yes, I want to send it!
You useless machine.

The ground of Utillia was terrifying.

Even the islands moved constantly to an offbeat that made Ki'b uneasy. She had tried to hide her discomfort from Khwaja Denvy and even Jarvis. Even though the long, golden horizon was before her, and she knew it was reality, a part of her was unable to comprehend what her eyes saw as truth. There were no trees. Bare. Barren. Not a tinge of green to match her skin. Was it the lack of roots that made the land unstable?

And yet the Kattamonts were so strong, thrusting through the burning-sea on their sand-ships of silver, surging over the dunes with fulsome ownership of all that lay around them. Ki'b tried to even out her breathing as she strove to keep pace with the wheelchair-bound female who rolled across the gravelled shoreline of the small island. It was no easy feat. Despite the wheelchair, the Kattamont was intimidating with her thick, muscled arms, covered in rosy fur. Her hands looked as though they would crush the wheels she manoeuvred with elegant ease.

Could she trust her saviours? Was there a possibility they were Twizels, tricking her into false hope and taking her back to a dark box? Ki'b frowned. If it was so, she did not believe they would have been so kindly, especially to Khwaja Denvy, and despite the discordance of the soil between her bare toes, there was a trusting thrum from the surface gravel. Even if she had never had the chance to grow up amongst her Kelib Sisters, and had been cast so far from the roots of her ancestors, she hoped that she could read the earth well enough to know they meant her family no harm.

She wiped aside a stray tear. Penny cried openly beside her, soft sobs of worry for Clive who lay in the lap of the wheelchair Kattamont. Reaching out, she took her sister's hand, squeezing it. Brown eyes sought hers, wide with fear. Ki'b hated that fear. It was crushing.

"There she is. Home."

Ki'b stirred at the voice of the wheelchair Kattamont and looked up. Home. It was a word Khwaja Denvy and Titus used when talking about the House of Flames. Penny used it often in reference to Tempath. None of them had ever said it with such honesty and conviction as had the Kattamont beside her. Ki'b covered her mouth against the gasp, her eyes drawn to the beautiful sight lying just off the beach.

Banked on the shoreline, gleaming under the last rays of the Sun, a sand-ship bobbed against the swelling waves of the burning-sea. She had seen the magnificent vessels before, in the distance, gliding along the tops of the dunes, but this one was within reach and overwhelmingly huge. Its hull appeared patched together with Zaprex metal of different gradients and strengths, shining spectra of light across the sand like coloured flowers over a meadow. The wings and the masts were transparent until creased and fluttered by the wind. It reminded her of a dragonfly, sitting upon the surface of a pond.

"It's so beautiful."

"She's called the *Lawless Child*. A nyhot. Medium class vessel."

Ki'b scrubbed back her hair. If the sand-ship before her was 'medium' sized, she could not begin to picture anything larger. As if guessing her thoughts, the Kattamont beside her laughed and ruffled her hair.

"You do not ever want to meet the giant navy sand-ships. But it is the cargo-ships that are the biggest. They are slow and huge. Oh. Their engines sing the most magnificent songs, though."

They started down the soft, grass-covered hill towards the *Lawless Child*. Ahead of them, the queen carried Khwaja Denvy. Crew from a small camp on the beach ran to meet them and Ki'b was entranced by the multicoloured array of Humans, Kelibs, and Kattamonts. Some of the Kelibs had tails, and some of the Humans had Kelib skin, and some of the Kattamonts had Human hands. She blinked at the strangeness of it all.

"We're a bit of a blended bunch."

"You're half-breeds," Ki'b murmured. Now the eerily Human hands of the lady beside her, rolling along in her wheelchair, were no longer a mystery. She looked different because she was.

"We're the castoffs no one wants." The Kattamont tipped her head to one side, shrugging.

Ki'b relaxed, sinking her feet deeper into the clover rich soil. The half-cast Kattamont was right. Home was the right word. Utillia was home.

"By the way," the Kattamont smiled, "I'm Nixlye, Princess of the Misfit Pride."

Heat tinged Ki'b's cheeks. "Ki'b…ah…Just Ki'b. This is Penny, and you are carrying Clive."

"And the old Kattamont?"

"Is our caretaker, Denvy Maz."

Nixlye nodded. "Mother should introduce herself, but it is unlikely she ever will; she tends to forget such formalities."

"Mother?"

"Term of respect. She is the birth-mother of my alpha-mate." Nixlye pointed at the shorter, silvery-toned Kattamont, firing orders at the crew ahead of them. "She is Zafiashid, Captain of the *Lawless Child*, Queen of the Misfits, Outcast of the Silvertide Pride."

Ki'b crinkled her nose. "That is a lot of titles."

Nixlye laughed. "I am sure she will add a few more to her name before she dies heroically in battle. Come, come. Let's get you all on board and checked out by the doctor."

Ki'b bounced on her heels. "Hear that Penny? Everything is all right. They have a healer!"

"But…Clive?" Penny bit her lip.

Ki'b hugged her tightly around the waist. "It will be all right. You will see."

She tugged on the Human girl, dragging her down the small knoll after the wheelchair's grooves. Khwaja Denvy might have a chance to live if they had a real healer on the sand-ship. She clutched at the hope rising within her, holding it tightly. She could always hope. Khwaja Denvy had taught her that.

If she had thought the sand-ship was huge from a distance, it was far bigger by the time they had climbed aboard. With no soil between her toes to feel the vibrations and drumbeat of the land a dizziness beset her on the metal and wooden planks of the deck. She swayed, a sickening pit forming in her stomach, bile threatening to rise to her mouth.

A hand steadied her and someone knelt by her side. He was a half-breed, skin wrinkled and old, but tattooed with pretty patterns from his cheeks, down his neck and arms. He draped a dangling chain, laden with rocks, around her neck. It took moments for the unsteadiness to settle and the distant drum beat to return. It no longer leaked through the soles of her feet. It echoed around her disconcertingly, seeming to resonate from rocks about her neck. She frowned, staring down at the necklace before looking up in confusion at the man kneeling beside her.

"Any better, love?"

"Yes, thank you," she muttered. "I thought the wood..." she stared down at the deck and curled her bare toes against the hardened surface.

He shook his head. "Long dead wood, Little Mountain Flower." The half-breed rubbed the banister sadly. "There has been no drumbeat in this wood for a long time."

He smiled, giving her head a pat. His hand was heavy but reassuring, the pressure steadfast like a mighty trunk, reminding her of Khwaja Denvy. In the dim evening light, his half-breed skin showed the touches of Human hair. That was the difference, she realized. He was hairy. A hairy Kelib man. Then she noticed his eyes. They were far too Human—warm, inviting, and a pale silver like Clive's. She bit her lip, hiding her giggle at the thought that he looked like Clive.

"Here in Utillia we Kelibs wear our soil around our necks. The princess tends to forget about it."

Ki'b looked up at the sound of Nixlye's wheelchair. The princess looked ashamed, with a flush on her Human cheeks. "I apologize! I am so used to thinking as a Kattamont."

The half-breed chuckled. "Well, we all choose one part of us to affiliate with. The sapling here is a pureblood, though, Princess. We'll need to keep an eye on her. They do tend to stick to islands more. If she's going to be on a sand-ship we might need to get a few more rocks around."

Ki'b touched the small stones on the chain. "Thank you, sir."

"Little Mountain Flower, if you need anything else at all, come see me. I'm first mate on this vessel." He waved her off. "You can make a rock-chain yourself when you get a chance."

"I will!" Beaming, Ki'b ran after Nixlye and Queen Zafiashid.

Strange buzzing lanterns lit the dark corridors of the sand-ship's interior. The smell was different to the oils Ki'b had once known, and she stared at the faintly burning liquid as she passed. Eventually, so deep down it seemed, the queen shoved open a door into a large cabin and heaved Khwaja Denvy inside. Ki'b quickly scurried through, dragging Penny behind her. She watched anxiously as the queen placed Khwaja Denvy's limp body onto a large bed. Queen Zafiashid groaned, rolling her shoulders.

"He might look like a sack of bones but he weighs as much as a baby usks[6] carcass," she griped. The queen crouched beside the bed

---

6 Usks – magnificent, large burning-sea-dwelling creature, rarely seen, but said to be good luck to sailors. Sometimes they get beached on islands, and their bones are used for building homes of island-dwellers.

and glanced back at Ki'b. "He must have been something to look at when he was healthy."

Ki'b frowned. There had never been much light in the box that had held them all. It had been hard to know what any of them had looked like in the beginning. Jarvis, Clive, and Penny's appearances, when they were all freed, had surprised her. She had known them for two sol-cycles but never seen their faces, only their voices that had soothed her fears in the darkness.

Queen Zafiashid snorted at her inability to reply and stood, approaching to scoop Clive from Nixlye's lap and settle him in a smaller cot.

"See what you can do about these pathetic things, Jythal. I will be top-deck."

Jythal? Who was Jythal?

Ki'b gasped as the queen brushed past and left the room, revealing the silent presence that had appeared in the cabin while her attention had been on the queen. Penny was gaping at the tall Kattamont that rivalled Khwaja Denvy in height. He was beautiful, but not in the way she thought Jarvis was handsome. Jarvis was broad, growing stronger and harder like a Kelib bone-blade being tempered by fire each day. The Kattamont looming over them was like her Mor-Mor's white silk scarves. She was taken back, spinning in the distant memories of the crackling firelight from the Family Halls, when her Mor-Mor and Sisters had danced with grace, their soft, flowing gowns rippling with the movement of water. It had been a long time since she had felt so much at home so quickly, and her bare toes curled against the wooden floor. The Kattamont smelt like the herbs that were bottled throughout the cabin, and the tip of his paws were stained with their sap. While Khwaja Denvy had layers of colour through his air-gills and fan-tail, this Kattamont was colourless, almost like a glittering apparition, one of the wandering spirits of the woods her Sisters and Mors had whispered about, like the white stag Kelib men always hunted but could never catch.

He stepped past her, toward Nixlye. Ki'b shrank back, feeling small beside the two giant creatures.

"What happened?" The male's voice was calm, vibrating with a low purr that rattled his air-gills.

"Mother and I found this old prince and these cubs being attacked by poachers. The prince has lost a lot of blood and the boy is badly bruised. You had best check his neck; his breathing is quite laboured."

Ki'b found her courage, moving to Khwaja Denvy's side.

"You have to help Khwaja Denvy! He is dying."

But the white Kattamont ignored her, speaking softly to Nixlye. "Poachers: Kelib or Human?"

"Kelib."

"Hmmm, the worst kind. No offense, little one." He patted Ki'b's head with a large paw as he passed her to crouch beside Clive's cot. The breath in her chest held fast. He fished through pouches attached to the belts around his waist, pulling out small stones and shells. He flung them out and they held their place, suspended over Clive, beginning to form a chain. Jythal netted his paws together in a series of movements.

Ki'b stepped back as a glow wrapped itself warmly around Clive's neck. Penny gasped, covering her mouth.

"Runes," she heard her Human sister mumble.

Runes? Clive had used, albeit rather poorly, the Old Way art several times. He claimed it was a skill only Sun Monks knew, and he had been training as a Sun Monk before the Twizels had sacked his Temple and taken him. How did a Kattamont know a Sun Monk art? Was it more than Humans tinkering with things they did not understand? She had been wrong, then, in her assumption. Perhaps it was more; perhaps it was a language—one she did not know. After all, it had taken her some time to learn the Human tongue inside the box to be able to talk to Jarvis, Clive, and Penny.

"You know of it?" Jythal gathered his sticks and stones in a paw.

"Not entirely. But…" Penny took Clive's hand. "Clive was going to be a Sun Monk. His father was a travelling bard, and could not look after him, so he left him at a Temple. But then…everything…went wrong…"

"I see."

Ki'b caught the narrowing of Jythal's lips as he stood, shifting towards her and Khwaja Denvy. She had to wonder what his Runes had told him about Clive, about his other injuries from captivity. Whatever was she supposed to tell these people, to explain their escape, and the reason they were even in Utillia? She rubbed her sweaty hands together, wishing for Jarvis and Master Titus.

Jythal's head turned her way, though his eyes stared over her, at nothing in particular.

"This prince—he is your guardian?"

Ki'b bit her lip. "Kind of. We have another with us: Master Titus. He and Jarvis are away at the moment."

"The poachers were after his fur, no doubt." Jythal was speaking to Nixlye, over her head.

"Whatever do you mean?" Nixlye snorted. "You cannot see him, Jythal. How do you know his fur colouring?"

Jythal smirked, rolling the Rune stones, sticks, and shells between his claws. "*Tah*, you have no confidence in me, dear heart."

"Is he special?" Ki'b gripped the arm of Nixlye's wheelchair.

A kind smile soothed her anxiety and she was drawn to Jythal's side as the large Kattamont knelt beside Khwaja Denvy, throwing his stones, sticks, and shells into the air once more. Nixlye settled both hands on her shoulders as they watched the light emanate from the old Kattamont's wounds.

"We have legends of a Gold Lion but we have always thought of them as just legends. There has never been a gold prince known amongst the Kattamont Prides."

Ki'b studied Khwaja Denvy. He had said nothing about his fur being different, or about being special to his people. Perhaps that was why he had not wanted to return to Utillia—because he was different.

"Interesting." Jythal settled back on his hind-legs, removing his paws from the yoke. "This metal appears to be quite lethal to him. Do you know what it is made of?"

"It is just metal," Ki'b told him, "but it is the enchantment on it that makes it dangerous to Khwaja Denvy. He is…" She covered her mouth.

"Khwaja Denvy is an Ageless One." Penny piped up from behind them.

Ki'b gasped, turning sharply towards her, where she sat on the cot that held Clive.

"Penny!"

"We have to tell someone. Master Titus isn't here. Khwaja Denvy needs help! They saved us from the poachers and they're obviously not Twizels."

"How do you know that?" Ki'b stamped her feet.

"Messengers?" Nixlye's hand squeezed her shoulder gently. "You're all Messengers."

Ki'b ducked her head, wishing she could hide behind her hair, but it had not grown out long enough yet. "We do not come from the House of Flames. Only Khwaja Denvy and Master Titus do. Twizels captured us in Pennadot. Khwaja Denvy was with us for a long time in a box. Until Master Titus saved us."

"How long?" Jythal's voice was soft.

Ki'b nibbled her bottom lip. "We're not really sure, but Khwaja Denvy thinks it might have been about two sol-cycles."

"There were more children." Penny hid her head in her hands. "And more boxes, but they didn't survive the journey. Khwaja Denvy kept us alive."

"Then in return," Jythal was tucking wads of heavily- scented, herb-encrusted pouches around the yoke, "we shall do everything we can to keep him alive."

Ki'b relaxed slightly, noticing Khwaja Denvy already looked far more settled than he had in months. "Thank you." She breathed out in relief.

"I may not be able to remove the yoke, little one, but a skilled Rune Wielder, I am. I should be able to dampen the effects of the enchantment enough to give him some peace."

"But the Twizel curse?" Penny slid down from Clive's cot. "Not even Master Titus could do anything about it."

Jythal dipped his head. "Know this, little Human—the power of something is in what you, yourself, give it. The best thing you can do for your guardian is trust that this foul thing has no grasp on him and, then, it no longer will have."

Penny's eyes widened. "Really?"

"Indeed." Nixlye wheeled closer to Penny, leaning forward. "Why, Zaprexes often used this very concept to protect their artefacts. It's a trick." She spread her strong, scarred hands. "If you think something dangerous will come, then something dangerous is likely to appear. But if you are a friend, and you believe you will come to no harm, then so it will be."

Ki'b smiled. "We know all about that."

"Must be an interesting story."

"Oh, it is, but it isn't my story to tell," Ki'b murmured shyly, thinking of Jarvis and the blue tinge to the skin of his arms as his body became metal. She often wondered if he thought he was cursed, too. It did not matter. She thought him brave, for he never complained about the gradual change beneath his skin, even though she could see it in his fingers whenever he touched her.

Jythal shifted back to Khwaja Denvy's side, casting out newly gathered stones of many colours and shapes. Ki'b noted the little leaves that danced amongst the circle haloing the old Kattamont.

"What are they going to do?" she queried.

"Well, you are a Kelib, so it is likely that the language of Runes would come naturally to you. You should be able to hear their songs and see what they are doing, with some study."

Ki'b brightened and joined the white Kattamont as Jythal knelt once more. "Runes act as a bridge between the Realms, a language we cannot speak, but one we can see. I believe it may be part of what the Zaprexes called the Song of Eternity, made into a physical, written language." Jythal tapped his nose. "The best way I can describe their work is that they stitch and knit bits of the Primary Realm with bits of the Secondary Realm."

"Make them whole again?" Ki'b whispered.

Jythal nodded. "Here they will deal with the lung infection and clear his air-gills." He started combing the matted bundles of Khwaja Denvy's mane.

"How do you know they will help?"

Jythal did not turn from his work. "Because I trust the Song of Eternity from which the Runes come. He will be fine. You'll see."

Ki'b bit her tongue. Was this the same thing Khwaja said when he told her not to give up hope? She squeezed her cheeks, wanting to tell the Kattamont he was attempting a silly task trying to brush Khwaja Denvy's mane. She had tried so often to deal with the wreck of the elderly beast's hair, but to no avail. He finally settled back with a scowl over his brow.

"I'm going to suggest that Mother shave his mane. It is causing considerable pain to him due to the yoke. It will be a shame but the skin is becoming inflamed and his air-gills infected. It caused his respiratory infection." Jythal set his utensils aside. "I do not want to do it, and I do not think you should either, Nixlye."

"Why not?" Ki'b looked from one to the other. "Can't you do it now?"

"I am a prince," Jythal scratched his chin, "but I am not part of the brotherhood of this elder. It would be inappropriate. Nixlye is my queen; she shouldn't be shaving any male's mane but her princes'. It tends to be a form of punishment, or humiliation. To make an unruly prince obey the Pride."

"Oh..." Ki'b shuffled on her feet. Unwillingly the foggy, blurred features of her Mor-Mor drifted into her mind. She recalled so little about her, but the distinct pattern of the woman's beautiful glowing tattoos stood out against the darkness of the home she had lost. Even so young, she knew they had not been for beauty, despite how beautiful they were to her innocent eyes.

"Don't worry." Jythal smiled. "It doesn't take too long to grow back, and it will make him look a bit younger. And it will definitely improve his health."

"You're right," Nixlye agreed. "It should be Mother. Technically she has no official pride and therefore no princes. She is an abnormality in the Prides. She should be able to help."

"She also doesn't believe in curses," Ki'b offered, trying to reassure herself.

"That's right." Nixlye laughed. "She doesn't." The princess clapped her hands together. "Now, I think you young ladies need some calming tea." Nixlye wheeled backwards, skilfully manoeuvring her chair around the tight room. Ki'b sank back against the bed. Tea sounded delightful.

"It is likely that we will stay docked until the scavengers return. We can go and search for your friends then. My mate will also be back and he is a great tracker." Nixlye put a pot to boil on a small stove.

Ki'b blinked back tears. She could not comprehend the relief that washed over her. Her head felt heavy and she rubbed her cheeks, pausing as she smudged blood from her cut hands over her skin. A tender paw caught her far smaller hand. Jythal crouched beside her. She wondered if he ever got tired of kneeling, but then remembered that she was actually very small, and she had to be unusual on the sand-ship. Everyone else around her was just huge.

A glow formed over the gooey wounds and shimmering Runes gathered, gradually sealing shut the cuts across her skin. The pain she had not, until now, noticed throbbing up her arms faded, and a tension in her shoulders eased. She looked up at Jythal, into the pink eyes that stared blankly over her in a glassy gaze. Ki'b frowned. They were not at all like Clive's silver Retenna eyes that had a clarity to them, full of blazing life. They were eyes that stared without seeing. Now she knew why he looked without looking.

"You're blind."

"You are very observant. Yes, I am."

"I am so sorry."

"Whatever are you apologizing for?" Jythal chuckled. "It is something people do tend to notice eventually. I don't mind." He rested a paw on his knee.

"I should not have been so rude."

"Everyone is rude." Jythal shrugged. "Even I am rude." He bent closer and whispered. "You are short."

Ki'b bit her lip, holding in a giggle.

Nixlye wheeled over, passing her a large cup of tea and throwing a blanket around her shoulders. She noted that Penny, too, was snuggled up warmly. She offered thanks and sipped the brew. Finally, after so long, they were safe. Khwaja Denvy was not going to die today, or tomorrow. She could breathe without a lump in her throat.

"Were you…born blind?" Ki'b played with the rim of her tea cup.

Jythal raised an eyebrow. "Were you born short?"

Ki'b pouted. "Yes. I'm a Kelib. And I'm not that short. You're just huge!"

He laughed at her. "I suppose I must be. But in answer to your question, no, I have not always been blind. My blindness is the result of forced exposure to the Sun." He held out his wrists and Ki'b stared. The fur had been rubbed back, no longer able to grow, revealing scars like her own, the ligature markings of shackles.

"I know what it is like to be kept in a cage."

"Poachers?" Ki'b choked out.

"He would be dead if it were poachers," Nixlye said. "Let me tell you, little one, that not all queens and princesses respect their rare princes."

"Rare? You're rare?" Ki'b twisted back to Jythal.

"I have no colour in my fur, my air-gills, or my fan-tail. It is a bit odd, yes?" Jythal smiled. "Also, it is horrible to keep clean."

"Very few princes are born amongst the Prides, let alone ones without colour." Nixlye took one of Jythal's paws and carefully placed it around a cup of tea.

"I have heard that I am rather like the Human Kimwyns, though we never get any of them across the Border."

"You would be right," Penny piped up. "They also have no colour. My father often said he thought the Sun stole their colour from them because they had slept with the daughters of the Stars."

Jythal guffawed. "I like that story. You'll have to tell me more."

Penny beamed. "I'd love to. Father had wonderful stories. I know so many of them!"

Ki'b treasured the smell of the bitter tea. It was reassuring and relaxing, though it could very well have been the presence of the tall Kattamont sitting beside her. "I am a white lion." He held out a paw. "The Zaprexes created the sky-sea not to harm our kind, but, with the destabilization of the Borders and the collapsing of the Secondary Realm, even here in Utillia we are not welcome any more. My eyes were taken from me by the Sun."

"But then…the Kimwyns…" Penny looked up from Clive's side. Ki'b knew what her Human sister feared. Coltarian's eruption was coming, and not even the sky-sea would survive. Her sister feared for her pale cousins.

"Be glad for the coming of the Long Night." Nixlye sighed. "The Sun will be less harsh."

"Indeed." Jythal smiled. "I do miss the outside world. My dreams are truly not enough. They are just dreams."

Ki'b blinked. That was a strange thing to say. It sounded rather like something Khwaja Denvy would say because he was a dream master. Was it possible? Had they found other dreamathic Kattamonts? Were all Kattamonts dreamathic?

Perhaps if they were dreamathic then she had found her way to safety.

Ki'b felt the warm tears begin to trickle down her cheeks, collecting under her chin. She could no longer hold them in and wear the brave mask she had so hoped to hold for Khwaja Denvy's sake. Was it too much to hope that they were finally safe, or was it a fool's hope?

"Oh, no, no, no, don't cry. Really, it is fine. I'm quite all right." Jythal touched her shoulder, but she shied away, shaking her head.

"No, it is not…it is just…I was so scared…and Khwaja Denvy told me it would all be all right and I did not believe him, and now you are here and it is all right but I am still scared." She sobbed against her dress sleeve.

"I think you have known only fear for such a long time. You may not even believe me when I tell you that you are safe now, Little Mountain Flower." Jythal wiped aside her tears with a large paw. "Of all the lands in the North, Utillia is the one place orphans will find a home."

Ki'b curled against his large arm, wondering if he truly meant his words—for would not all of her people become orphans when the sky-sea collapsed and Pennadot's forests burned?

Would they find a home in Utillia too?

PRINCE JYTHAL OF THE MISFIT PRIDE

CHAPTER SIX

01000100 01101111 00100000 01101110 01101111 01110100
00100000 01110011 01110000 01100101 01100001 01101011
00100000 01101111 01100110 00100000 01110100 01101000
01100101 00100000 01001011 01100101 01111001 00100000
01110011 01101111 00100000 01100110 01110010 01100101
01100101 01101100 01111001 00101110 00100000 01010100
01101000 01100101 01111001 00100000 01100011 01101111
01110101 01101100 01100100 00100000 01100010 01100101
00100000 01101100 01101001 01110011 01110100 01100101
01101110 01101001 01101110 01100111 00101110

NORTHERN TOWER – PRIVATE COMMUNICATION LINKAGE –
01010011 01100101 01101011 01101000 01101101 01100101 01110100

The remains of the happy little camp Jarvis had left earlier that morning was strewn around his feet. His optical analysis came up with nothing as he scanned the globular trees by the lagoon, searching for any sign of life. The damage to his systems prohibited a deeper search. He knelt, fingers trembling as he picked up Ki'b's herbal kit. He had bought the little boxes for her at the border town between Pennadot and Utillia, and the delight on her face had been brighter than any Sunrise. Now they were slick with blue-tinted blood. It had to be Khwaja Denvy's.

Carefully he pieced the kit back together, stowing it in his hip-bags.

The thought of his orphan siblings alone and hurt again—he wanted to panic, to rush around, calling out their names. But none of it would help. That much he had learnt. Panicking would be of no aid to anyone and, besides, he could barely stand.

On shaking legs, he heaved himself to his feet, crossing wearily to where Titus crouched over a slain Kelib. Jarvis covered his mouth and nose at the foul stench emanating from the corpse.

"Surely the bodies haven't started decomposing already?" he muttered.

"Actually they're…" Titus plucked at the leathery shirt the Kelib male wore. "Cannibals."

Jarvis's mouth went dry. Without Khwaja Denvy's presence in their little prison perhaps even he—Jarvis shook his head—no—he had promised he would stop thinking this way. The moment they had broken out of the box, and light had flooded his eyes once more, he had been reborn. He was not that boy in a box anymore.

"We call them poachers." Aaldryn approached, dragging another corpse along behind him. He flung it over the other. "They're utter scum. You mentioned you have an Obilb in your family? And your old Kattamont is golden furred?"

Jarvis nodded.

"Rythrya Stones be blessed there were only three poachers. They usually hunt in far larger packs." Aaldryn glanced around with a frown. "They can take down a Kattamont queen if they're in the mood, and I have heard of them killing brotherhoods for sport."

"Why?" Jarvis spluttered out.

"Our fur. Our tail feathers. Also, apparently there is some kind of trade with the Batitics for our…ah…hmmm…" Aaldryn rubbed his chin. "Maybe I'll tell you about it later."

Jarvis paled. "I don't think I even want to know!"

"Perhaps not."

Jarvis pointed at the dead poachers with his good arm. "But they're wearing Human skins."

Aaldryn shrugged. "Of course. Humans are far easier to kill. Obilb skin is highly prized. Very, very pretty."

Jarvis grabbed Titus' arm. "Penny!"

"Don't worry." Aaldryn kicked over one of the bodies, revealing an arrow. It had to be nearly the length of Jarvis' arm. It was fletched with the same bright azure feathers as Aaldryn's tail. The Kattamont grinned.

"This belongs to my mate. I provide the tail feathers for her arrows. It is likely your family were taken back to our sand-ship. They will be safe with my Mother and my mate. She said our sand-ship is docked off the island—likely around the other side, away from the null-zone."

"But all the blood." Jarvis gestured to the patch in the clover-grass. "It belongs to Khwaja Denvy!"

Titus touched his shoulder, trying to urge him to calm. But he simply could not still his racing heartbeat. Something had triggered it and sweat was pooling in the nape of his neck.

"Yeh know the old man, Little Weasel. He's lived a long life. If he knows he has children ta safeguard, he'll always keep fighting."

Jarvis bowed his head. It was true. Khwaja Denvy seemed to have no choice but to try and protect them. It was part of his nature. Titus moved off to collect Penny and Clive's packs, but he heard his master mutter.

"Besides, the old man has far too much Zaprex in him ta abandon anyone by dying."

Jarvis rubbed the scar across his arm where the protector bot had savagely slashed him and contaminated him with philepcon liquid. He understood the drive, the intense desire, the need to protect.

He could not deny how very Zaprex it was.

The walk across the small island should not have been difficult, not compared to scaling the heights of the Ovin-tu Mountains in a blizzard, but Jarvis felt himself lagging with each step, his heart racing in overdrive, sweat collecting under his collar. His feet slipped beneath him. Red warning signals flickered across his optical screens as his vision fizzed. He gritted his teeth, ignoring the annoying flashes to focus on Titus ahead of him. The bleeding hole in his chest ached and throbbed, but surely it was fine—his master had patched it up.

Or—maybe it was not all right.

The single thought froze in his mind.

Blaring, sharp pain speared up his spine, snapping every limb into a tight lock and Jarvis felt himself drop. Had he hit something solid, not soft grass, he was sure he would have sounded metallic, landing with a heavy clunk.

"Jarvis!" Titus' voice was a sharp twang through his skull. "Holy Sun, Jarvis!"

He sensed his master over him, soon joined by Aaldryn. He was pretty sure he grumbled something out, actually he must have sworn, for a moment later his ear was boxed sharply by his master.

"Don' yeh use that language on me!"

That was rich, coming from his foul-mouthed master.

"You should have said something earlier." Aaldryn began to cut through his shirt, tugging at the bandage. "Pushing yourself only makes things worse." The Kattamont pulled out a new wad of sticky padding from the medical kit before pouring something over the bleeding wound, something that made it burn. Jarvis sat up abruptly.

"Holy Sun!"

Titus pushed him back down. "We have ta clean the wound again."

"I don't care! You're making it worse."

Aaldryn slapped the patch across the hole in his chest. "For someone with a bullet wedged in one of his lungs, you're doing a lot of yelling." Aaldryn turned to Titus. "We have to get the bullet out. There is no telling how much longer the philepcon liquid is going to keep flooding the system. I had hoped it might dissolve, but it doesn't look like it will."

"Can you do that?" Titus had a vice grip on Jarvis' shoulders, though Jarvis doubted he could move even if he wished to. Aaldryn should not have mentioned his lung. Now that he focused on it, he could feel the little piece of metal, sitting there, wedged inside his chest and it was making everything scream.

"No, I can't," Aaldryn was still talking, "but my blood-brother is a Rune Doctor. He should be able to do something about this."

Jarvis groaned in protest as Titus lifted him, cradling him against his chest.

"He better be good, this blood-brother of yours."

Aaldryn's foot-paws sounded ahead of them. "He's the best doctor you'll ever find."

"Put me down," Jarvis protested weakly.

Titus glared at him. "Learn ta accept help when yeh get it, laddie. It won' always be there."

TITUS TIMOTHY TELVON - MESSENGER HUNTER

CHAPTER SEVEN

As you sit upon your high throne,
watching jigsaw pieces of lands
fit together, do you ever wonder
what we little ants are doing down
below you?

Private Communications Link.
Utillian Time 1:05AM.
Signal: Weak.
Upload: Completed.
Do you wish to send?

Denvy had not been able to dream since the yoke had been firmly locked around his neck. It had drained him of all dreamathic abilities. The darkness of sleep had become a bottomless pit of empty noth-ingness that swaddled him like a choking death. He despised this lonely, hollow, echoing, dreamless sleep. Always his dreams had over-flowed with the rolling of faces from his long past. He wandered the bright sunlight-filled halls of his childhood. Therein the welcoming arms of his family waited. Dreams were the eternal escape from reality, to a peaceful time of harmony, when songs had ruled the Lands of Livila.

He knew now that he was asleep; a dreamathic was always aware of sleep, even if there was no dream to be had. Through the veil of slumber, he could feel the ache of stiff limbs. Skin was on fire. Yet as he drifted through the black tar, a dot kept appearing.

It was a mere speck in the ocean of sludge-sleep, blinking on and off, but it should not have been there with the yoke on. He could not dream; even a little white dot in a sea of nothing was a dream.

He stepped towards it, one foot-paw at a time. With each step he grew lighter. The burden around his neck became lighter, and the burning sensation down his back eased until it was entirely gone. As they had been in his youth, his muscles became flexible and his bones less brittle. Denvy stirred, fluttering his eyelids. They were not caked shut by conjunctivitis. His lungs were unburdened with mucus, no longer crackling with illness. He beamed brightly, studying himself in the reflection of the glossy floor beneath his foot-paws. A childish, very cubby face looked back at him. He was barely old enough to have been more than a decade past his birth. He was a cub! How delightful a dream this was. Denvy chuckled, prancing down a long hall until he skidded to a sudden stop in alarm.

He was in a familiar world. This was the world of his past—the vast, sprawling city of Tikal. His people had called Tikal, The Rainbow City, and truly it was a place of dancing light. The endless arching windows, bejewelled with colours, dazzling white reflective floors and pillars of glass. Interlinking towers and walkways entwined like the webs of giant spiders. Only here there were no spiders, but, instead, little Zaprex ants scampered about.

Denvy frowned.

His fur spiked around his neck as he finally felt the presence nearby. The mere tingling it sent against his skin triggered a flood of awe, love, and hope as he smelt the soft scent of lilies. A faint static discharge nibbled against his foot-paws as the floor beneath him rippled due to a Zaprex's wings releasing their excess energy. Denvy's lips parted. Gradually he dared to turn. He had to know—

He had to know if his dream had kept the image of the one who had created him.

Could he still recall the Zaprex who had given him the spark of life?

Across the long hall, a lone figure sat upon a futon, dressed in a simple blue chiton, patterned with azure lilies.

"Nefertem," Denvy murmured.

He had disturbed the Zaprex with his glee, and a rather amused face was now studying him. Stunning sapphire eyes danced with mirth. Denvy felt his limbs slacken. They were exactly as they should have been—old, weary, but ever welcoming in the silver-tinged features of the delicate fairy.

"Maahes, whatever brings you here?" Nefertem set down the tattered book it had been reading, one nimble finger tracing the worn brown paper as though the tome was precious. In the light from the towering window, the graceful Zaprex's semi-transparent chiton constantly changed colour, mimicking the surrounds. "I thought you were playing with the other cubs who came up from the surface? Hazanin organized the whole thing for your hatching-day."

Denvy crinkled his nose. Hatching-day. Yes. That was what Zaprexes called their day-of-birth, but he had no recollection of this particular memory, or this dream. He slackened, staring around at the vast hall, empty of all but him and his creator.

"Maahes, is everything all right?" Nefertem's body whirred as it floated up from the seat. Ethereal wings expanded, flowing freely in strands of glossy energy. On slender heels, Nefertem landed beside him, barely reaching him mid-waist. Long ears twitched rearward in enquiry, though the smile he received was tender. It terrified him.

Nefertem should not have been smiling.

Nefertem should have been weeping. Everything the fairy loved, everything the fairy had worked for, was decaying and falling to ruins. Denvy squeezed his paws tightly. This Nefertem was a dream of a time before the Thousand Sol-cycle War. It did not know of the horrors to come.

"I think I am lost, Gifu," Denvy whispered.

"Lost?" Nefertem blinked, expression flipping from a pleasant glow to a calculating frown for a brief moment. It lifted his paw and gave it a gentle pat.

"Mayhap something has gone awry in your navigational software. I shall have a look this evening during your hibernation." Nefertem turned, tugging gently on his paw. "Come along. We cannot get lost in our own home, can we? Walk with me."

The stroll was slow, for Nefertem's steps were far shorter than his long strides, and he tried to compensate for the elegant Zaprex. They stopped constantly to allow Nefertem to engage in conversation with the patrons of the glowing halls and high walkways. It was the noise that confused him. It was like wind through a forest, only the forest was far below them, deep in the bowels of the city's inner sanctum. After passing another dozen Zaprexes, chatting happily and breaking his heart with their impish smiles, the noise intensified. He had not heard it for so long it was no wonder he had forgotten the sound. The dream he had conjured up was so accurate it had even recreated the buzzing hive melody of Zaprexes all dwelling in one hub. Hearing the harmony almost made him lose his footing beside Nefertem.

His foot-paws halted and he stood limply, allowing the song to seep deeply into his core. Tears trickled down his cheeks. He had forgotten what it had been like to be connected to such an immense symphony. For so long, it had just been him, Hazanin, and a few of the Ancient Ones who held on to the vagueness of hope. And their combined melodies were so weak.

This was true harmony—what the Zaprexes did best.

"Everyone dies," he choked out weakly.

"The Sun sets on every Empire, Maahes. It will even set on ours." Nefertem's hand curled into his fur.

"No, you don't understand Gifu. Everyone dies. I lose everyone."

"When you are lost, what do you do?"

Denvy frowned. The Zaprex's tone was gentle and yet urging as though tugging his mind in the direction it needed to turn. He stared out across the scene he had long forgotten; even in his dreams it had been vague and blurred. Never was it this crisp.

"You find your way home," he murmured.

"Yes." Nefertem nodded. "You find your way home. Denvy. It is time for you to go home. Your home needs you. It is calling you, across time and space, drawing you in, even if you have not yet realised it."

The overwhelming flood of emotion took him by surprise. Through his foot-paws, a dreamathic bond of immense power bombarded him. His fur stood on end and his fan-tail expanded to full frill at the familiar gush of love and warmth as Tikal's artificial intelligence made a mental connection deep inside his mind. A knitted web filled the hole the yoke had torn open, and, so faintly, he could see a flicker of dreamathic threads surrounding him.

He was actually here. Denvy staggered back, his breaths coming in sudden, sharp gasps as he struggled to take in the real, fresh, untainted air. The Dragon still slumbered in this world. The Zaprexes still ruled. They were healing the shattered planet piece by piece. The Towers were brimming with life. He was home, before the Thousand Sol-cycle War.

Twisting sharply, Denvy stared down at Nefertem.

"This is impossible. I'm home. I'm home?"

Nefertem's hands curled behind its back. "Hazanin must be dead in the future if Time is rippling. Interesting. I suppose that means the cycle is broken in the future. Troubling, but not unexpected from Sehkmet's calculations." The Zaprex twirled about. A door to the side of the hall opened, revealing an outside balcony. He followed the fairy through the entrance, blinking in the sunshine. Raising a paw to shade his eyes, Denvy watched sky-ships glittering in the rosy pink sunset across the sky-sea. His hearts raced at the sight and he wanted to vault over the edge of the boulevard. But he could not join them. He could not fly with them. This was not his time.

"How am I here?"

Nefertem shrugged. "It is likely that, in the future, the mainframe of the Northlands is being reset and you are being caught up in a reality ripple. I'd expect a few hiccups to happen if it's a single sector reset and not a full world-system reinstall. Even then, I couldn't hope for a hundred percent wipe out of the old desktop and mainframe."

Denvy ruffled his air-gills. He had to trust that Nefertem was correct. After all it was the scientist behind the sector-gods and the sectors of the Lands of Livila. While it might not have created the actual Towers, it was the combined Pantheon themselves that had built the software within them. His creator and Hazanin had been the two Zaprexes remaining who had devised the plan to pull the Northlands together, creating its rotational spin to replace the Towers.

"Why am I here?"

"You said you are lost; you have found your way home." Nefertem joined him, taking out its book as it seated itself on a nearby seat. "I think your consciousness is trying to tell you something."

Denvy opened his mouth. Nefertem lifted a hand, stalling his words before they escaped his mouth.

"My dear Maahes, you know very well that telling me anything now will not change your reality. It will simply change a reality that is not yours. Your past has already happened, my future has not. They cannot merge."

Denvy slumped into the seat beside the fairy. "Everyone dies…"

"You don't." Nefertem pressed a kiss to his forehead. "And, therefore, my song lives on in you, my dear son. Hold on to that."

CHAPTER EIGHT

As you sit surrounded by your mirrors,
which reflect your true nature, do you
ever wonder what I do as I sit up here
watching a world burn?

NORTHERN TOWER – PRIVATE COMMUNICATION LINKAGE –
01010011 01100101 01101011 01101000 01101101 01100101 01110100

The touch had been gentle, sending Denvy drifting back to a time he could barely recall. A hazy place in his mountains of memories stored on top of each other, weighing each other down until they were so compressed he could no longer bother remembering his youth.

But the touch and the sweet tender voice that accompanied it comforted him more than the pressure of the blankets and the warmth of a bed made for the heavy structure of his body. Denvy drifted in and out of the freedom of sleep, the deepest sleep he had settled into since his capture, and always the presence was behind him, the touch and the voice.

Gradually layers peeled back, fold by fold, and he woke. Precious life flowed through his limbs, and, while it was not the return to his immortality, he could feel his base program gradually beginning to repair itself. That meant the nano-bots in his body had regained function. Denvy sank deeper into the bed. It creaked and he relished the sound. Blankets slid off as he lazily raised an arm and scratched behind an ear.

He paused.

His lips parted. "Oh no."

His mane was gone. Denvy felt his head, his still-aching chest heaving in mild panic as he had the horrible thought that his air-gills were also missing, but he finally encountered the frilled gills and relaxed slightly.

So, it was only his matted mane that had been removed, the crown of a prince's glory. He had never been one for vanity, but deep down he was still a Kattamont prince. He had been a bit proud of his shaggy golden locks.

He stared at the ceiling and the lantern dangling above him, swaying back and forth. The scale of everything surrounding him was designed around something the size of a large Kattamont like himself. Sickly sweet scents lingered in the air and in the blankets. It had seeped into the wooden walls and floors—the aroma of a female Kattamont, and, by the intensity of it, a queen. He was in the quarters and the bed of a queen—with his mane shaved off.

Denvy crinkled his brow at the thought. Considering his size he doubted there had been any other place to put him, but he could not recall a queen ever giving up her quarters for a saggy old prince.

Had Utillian traditions changed in his centuries of self-imposed exile?

And had she—

Had she shaved off his mane?

"That'd be nice," he grumbled. "Always did hate tradition."

Still, he shuddered to think of what he looked like without the golden layers of his cascading hair and beard. He ran his paw over his chin. Some relief returned as he felt that whoever had given him a shave had left at least a small sampling for him to fuss over.

Worry not, old one. Mother has good taste. A dreamathic giggle tickled the edges of his mind.

He almost sat up in alarm, but his wasted muscles barely raised him from the pillows. It had been so long since he had felt anything remotely dreamathic. It was almost painful to bear and he rubbed his temples as he rolled himself from the heavy covers. Weakly he cast them aside. No one was in the dimly lit room. Outside the small pot-hole window, the sky-sea was a dull haze. It would never grow as dark in Utillia from the Long Night that fell across the Northlands, for the burning-sea reflected an enormous amount of light and heat into the sky-sea, which reflected light back, like two mirrors facing each other. But the Long Night was approaching. He could feel it in his bones. The Northlands was changing its tilt. The spin was slowing. Would this then be the last time the Northlands spun? Had the patch Nefertem tried to install, joining all the lands of the north together to keep Livila alive for just a little longer, finally run its course? He hated to think so, but it was possible that this was to be the Long Night that ended it all.

The dreamathic giggle caused him to lift his head once more. His eyes sought the door and he frowned. It was open slightly. An invitation for him to leave the cabin, if he could manage it.

Setting his teeth in a snarl, Denvy heaved himself up, wobbling on his legs. Rather more swiftly than he anticipated the nearest wall impacted his shoulder and he supported himself against it. Gradually he made his way out into the corridors beyond, keeping slow and steady on his foot-paws. He was on a sand-ship, that much he could deduce by the swaying, and the rich smell of processed Mist being channelled through powerful thrusters somewhere deep within the engines churning below. It was a distinct scent that reminded him of old, vicious days of warfare, bloodshed, and pride against pride. With a paw upon the rough surface of the timber corridor, he followed the pattern of the mind that was calling him, whispering with soft, fluttering touches. Onward through winding, intersecting passageways he staggered, until he felt the sudden strength of a powerful wind gusting down the corridor.

Denvy's air-gills spread in surprise. He hissed, releasing the thick feathers down the spine of his tail and he turned to encounter the familiar head of a burning wind far more ancient than even he was. Only he did not meet the shifty shape of something out of his past, coming to haunt him in jest to test his sanity. Instead a youthful prince was slumped against the wall, studying him with thoughtful azure eyes.

Teal-coloured air-gills and fan-tail feathers lay flat in submission to his superior age. Despite his strangely limp posture, the youth was showing subservience—apart from his hard, clear eyes. The pure ebony pelt, glossed with a silver lining, revealed a true descendent of the Silvertide Pride. Denvy straightened as best he was able, trying to overcome the pressure within the passageway as it continued to build.

"Denvy Maz, Dream Master of the Northlands of Livila, it really has been a while. So perhaps I should call you Maahes, yes?"

Denvy frowned. "Do I know you?"

"Oh, yes." The prince gave an awkward bow. "Forgive me for not introducing myself. You would not recognize me. I blended myself into this child's body. You would remember me as Khamsin, Titan of the North Wind."

"By the Almighty Sun." Denvy landed against the nearest wall. "Impossible. You perished. The Dragon threw all the Titans into the Unknown Realm and sealed you therein."

Khamsin shook his head. "It was a frightening battle of Elemental forces, indeed. I daresay it took out half this world with it, but I ran away before it truly began. I admit I was a coward, but I lived to fight another day."

Denvy scrubbed at his stubble beard, studying the young Kattamont. "So you will fight?'

"This child I inhabit has a strong will of his own. If he desires to do something then I will follow him and act accordingly. It was our pact. He provides me with energy to exist in this Realm, and I sustain his existence. He was born dead, Denvy. This land is tainted by the Zaprex waste." Khamsin sounded weary. "Something terrible has befallen Utillia—"

"The Zaprex crystals are growing out of their containment fields, aren't they?"

Khamsin snapped his head up, a momentary delay before surprise graced the young features of his host. "Yes. They are. How did you guess that? It took my children so long to figure that out, and they have been here for centuries."

Denvy shrugged. "I was raised amongst Zaprexes. Their technology is not unknown to me. You mentioned your children. Am I to presume then that the Simoon have entered the Primary Realm, like the Thyrrhos of Prometheus?"

Khamsin clicked his tongue. "They followed the Thyrrhos, yes, but I have not been leading them as my sibling leads her people. Until recently I did not know of my children's suffering here in Utillia."

"Suffering?" Denvy stepped back a pace.

"Yes." Khamsin hissed. "I desire to discover why my children are being enslaved by the Kattamonts, and, in repayment for saving her precious son, Zafiashid, Outcast of the Silvertide Pride, will save my children." Khamsin chuckled. "She does not believe in curses." His arm jerked outwards and he roughly bumped open the door beside him. "What better queen to have on your side than a queen brave enough to spit in the face of an Elemental Titan?"

"I suppose so," Denvy muttered as he followed Khamsin through the entrance, pausing on the threshold of a homely cabin that reminded him more of the interior of a small home than anything aboard a sand-ship. Warmth emanated from a stove beside a bench covered in cooking utensils and healing kits. Pots and pans hung from the ceiling, along with dangling lanterns.

A table was bolted tightly to the floor, along with the bookshelves, closed in to keep the books stored therein secure against the rocking and tossing of the sand-ship. The large bed was fit for a small pride, as wide as it was long. Denvy studied Khamsin's host. The young Kattamont prince looked as though he had reached his mature height, and barely reached Denvy's shoulders, therefore it was the startlingly pale, albino prince whom everything in the cabin was heighted for. Denvy smiled at the tall and graceful male who matched his own towering figure and rarity in fur tone. He sat on the bed's side, tending to a sight that made his hearts beat lightly in relief. Jarvis. Dear sweet little Jarvis was bundled under the blankets.

Denvy scanned the room, catching what he had missed. Ki'b lay in a small cot by the heat of the stove. He should have known she would not have been far from Jarvis' side.

A princess seated in a chair waved. "Khamsin, you may go." Khamsin bowed and Denvy watched in fascination as the body of the young Kattamont shifted its stance, the change in personality shown in the face as it relaxed. He glanced at Denvy with a sheepish smile.

"I apologise, sir. Khamsin wanted to greet you. He said you were old…friends?"

"Friends is a bit of a stretch, but perhaps now that can happen. Time tends to change even Elementals." Denvy chuckled. As unexpected as it was to find another Titan still in existence, it was not unwelcome. The Thousand Sol-cycle War had changed all Livila, and all those who dwelt upon her, and perhaps even the Elementals had realized their grave and terrible mistake.

The young prince inclined his head. "I am Prince Aaldryn, the alpha of our pride. Allow me to introduce you to my blood-brother, Jythal, and our queen, Nixlye."

So that explained why their little cabin was set out in such a manner—they were a pride, and the princess was not a neutral waiting to be a queen.

She was already a queen.

A very young queen, who presented herself as a neutral princess to the world outside of their little cabin. He was being honoured, as an elderly prince, to be permitted into their sanctuary.

Nixlye wheeled her chair towards him and he offered his paw for her to scent. Her colours were as beautiful as he remembered them, even distracted and overwhelmed as he had been by the poachers. Soft pink fur, and a tail full of lavender and white feathers. The hues were delicately pastel, alluring a watcher into a false sense of calm. Whatever confined her to the wheelchair lay hidden under layers of homespun blankets.

"I am glad to see you up and about. You had us worried."

She took his paw, rubbing it to her cheek.

"I do apologise for appearing before you in such a dishevelled state." He touched his chest. The ache of infection still wrapped itself about his throat, and fatigue was creeping into his limbs. Nixlye motioned him quickly into a nearby chair. She shook her head and clasped his paw tightly.

"Please! Sir, you are the guest amongst us. Even without a mane, you are the proudest looking prince in all Utillia."

"Hey!" Aaldryn's air-gills puffed out.

Nixlye waved dismissively at the young alpha. "Admit it: you have never seen a Gold Lion either."

Aaldryn snorted. "Fine, fine. That is new." He headed for the kitchen bench. Denvy heard him noisily fill a kettle, but his eyes remained firmly fixed upon the hand that held his paw. Once he would have been in awe at how small it was compared to his own, or how strong its grip was due to his weakened state. None of that mattered. It was a Human-shaped hand, with the vice grip of a Kattamont and soft, rosy fur spreading to fingers tipped with slender, bladed nails. The little queen had no air-gills, but her magnificent tail lay across the blanket spread over her lap.

"A half-breed," Denvy murmured. "That should be impossible."

The smile he received in return was surprisingly sad and her free hand squeezed against the blanket across her lap that bunched against her hidden legs.

"You are going to find that many things have changed in Utillia." Nixlye released his paw. "It may take some time for you to understand that."

He frowned. If the poachers they had encountered were anything to go by, then she was correct about that. But a Kattamont crossed with a Human—that was unimaginable, and yet she sat across from him. He could not deny her existence. What had happened to his land in his absence? His stomach twisted.

Denvy crinkled his brow, turning away. The little queen in the wheelchair had aided in dispatching the poachers, but she was not the one he remembered. She did not smell like the queen who had been in his presence, who had clipped off his mane.

"Who was it who carried me?"

"That would be Mother," Aaldryn said from his station by the kitchen bench. "Though no doubt she would prefer *you* call her Zafiashid. She is an exiled queen."

"I did not think such—"

"They do exist." Nixlye bit her lip. "Mother has survived this long because she has vengeance in her blood. She desires to take back the Silvertide Pride, and her rightful place as its Queen. If anyone can do it, it is Mother."

"But, yes, lone queens are unusual and unpredictable." It was Jythal who spoke, his gaze vacant. "A queen needs a pride as much as a prince needs a brotherhood. Kattamonts must have families." He stroked Jarvis' hair aside from his sweating temples and reached for a cloth. Denvy watched as the young Kattamont removed a rough stone from a nearby bench and it broke into a scattering of water, wetting the cloth with a sweet-smelling liquid. Jythal settled the cloth across Jarvis' neck.

"A Rune Wielder." Denvy touched his chest, feeling the rumbling thrum of the slowly healing infection therein. "Do I have you to thank for my improved health?"

Jythal bobbed his head, causing his white air-gills to spread slightly. "When I joined the crew of the *Lawless Child* I became their doctor. I much prefer using my skills for healing."

Denvy narrowed his lips, not wanting to imagine what else the Kattamont prince might have used his skills for. He paused his thoughts as Aaldryn handed him a cup, steaming with tea. He nodded his thanks.

"Runes are barely used in his era. It is hardly even known amongst the Sun Monks of Pennadot. Forgive me, but I find it incredibly difficult to understand how a blind Kattamont could be using the language of the Elementals."

Jythal turned his head aside. "It is a woeful tale, sir. Maybe I shall tell it to you someday, when my courage returns to me."

"I hope so." He could understand the hesitation. It was unlikely the young prince had been born blind, and it was doubtful his story was pleasant if it involved the loss of his sight.

The cup in his paws was warm, its scent of peppermint and lemon calming on his aching bones. He sipped the hot brew. The luxury. It felt like centuries since he had last tasted something so divine.

I am glad we can bring you cheer again. It would seem you have all been through much to stumble your way into Utillia. Lavender and pink coloured his mind, mixed with the touches of cotton wool, soft but just rough enough to itch. Denvy could not stop himself; he chuckled as he graced Nixlye with a fond smile. She mirrored it as her hands picked at the blankets bundled around her lap. No doubt they were all handmade, giving her mind the touch of the homespun mother despite the lioness boiling deep within.

"A dreamathic." Denvy set his tea down. "I have not heard a dreamathic voice in so many sol-cycles."

"So you *can* hear me." Nixlye beamed. "I told you he could hear me, Jythal."

Jythal snorted.

Nixlye touched her chest. "I've been able to speak to Jythal since I first met him, but we have to be wearing a particular sort of…" She pulled out a necklace from under the thick scarf she wore, holding out the chipped rock that hung off one end. It looked plain from the outside, barely noteworthy as a jewel, but she turned it slowly, revealing the geode, glittering in the lights of the lanterns.

"Ah, I see now." Denvy nodded. He picked at the yoke still stiff about his neck until the leather strap under it came loose, and with it, a string of similar jewels fell against his chest.

"So that explains how your mental voice can penetrate the yoke's barrier. You've made your own dreamathic network. Very, very clever."

"We have?" Nixlye blinked rapidly.

Denvy glanced from the young queen to Jythal. They had no idea what they had done. Interesting. They were running entirely off instinct. He wished some Messengers in Coltarian had as much initiative.

"I just thought it might help. I do not know much about dreamathics, other than what I read in the Iposti Archives, but these rocks have always helped Jythal and me. The little Kelib girl, Ki'b, said you were a Dream Master."

It was the way she said it—*Dream Master*—that made him chuckle. He had not heard his title said with such reverence in a long time.

It made him sound overly important and puffed up.

"I am. Well, I would be, if this—" he tugged at the yoke, "—wasn't here. Dreamathics come in classes. Those who are of the minor classes can communicate through the Secondary Realm's network, often using, as you have discovered, gem resonators, to increase their range and kinetic strength. The dreamathic Messengers who are born under the birth elemental gift of diamond have established a nexus of communication across the Plains of Blazing Fire. One could say they hijacked the old Zaprex crystal network and made it their own. It is something rather amazing to use if you ever get the chance." Denvy sighed wearily. "The mid-level classes can submerge themselves into the Secondary Realm, but cannot affect the Primary Realm through it. It is the high-level class you want if you desire to manipulate dreams into reality."

"And you're a high-level class?" Nixlye asked.

"No." Denvy shook his head. "I am a Dream Master. I accept that dreams *are* reality. There is a difference." He held up his tea cup. "Some folk never figure out what it is."

"So…" Jythal leant forward curiously, "did Nixlye and I accidently discover a dreamathic nexus then?"

"Most dreamathics are naturally drawn to things that will boost their projection fields. You were simply doing what was inbuilt into you, and by providing me with these gems you have widened my field a little, at least enough to join your nexus." He motioned to Aaldryn. "I take it you are not dreamathic?"

The prince grunted, though it was neither out of spite nor disgust. It held an air of fondness as he touched a paw to Nixlye's shoulder. "One voice in my head is enough for me. I am but a humble warrior-scribe who seeks the treasures *they* dream of."

"And we love you for it." Jythal offered from the bedside.

"You'd better," Aaldryn retorted, marching to his blood-brother's side and lounging lazily over his shoulder. His tail twirled anxiously as his gaze settled on Jarvis.

"He looks worse than when I brought him to you."

"That is just the fever of his remaining Human side. It must be discolouring his skin."

Aaldryn leapt back in surprise as Jarvis sat up with a shout. Denvy contained his alarm as Jythal lost his balance, ending up on the floor. Aaldryn ignored his blood-brother, bouncing over him elegantly and landing beside the distraught Jarvis to hold him down firmly. The young alpha's air-gills were flat against his back and neck, usually a sign of yielding. Yet, in his case, Denvy was sure it was to hide them away, to try and appear as kindly and unthreatening as possible. The alpha, it seemed, was dealing with Jarvis as though he were simply another blood-brother prince.

Denvy rose, aiding Jythal to stand. He noticed the strain in

Aaldryn's arms as he held Jarvis back against the bed, as if Jarvis' strength was uncontrollable in his panicked state.

"Whoa, whoa, it is all right, Jarvis. You are safe."

"Master Titus?" Jarvis choked.

"He's fine. He's resting with your brother Clive and sister Penny. Or…brooding. Maybe brooding is a better word. I think he is rather sore about losing that monster."

"Yes. Yes. He would be." The boy groaned, sinking back into the bed. "My head hurts."

"That is not surprising," Jythal said. "You are very dehydrated. Here, drink this. See if you can keep the tonic down now. You kept throwing it up before." Jythal carefully lifted Jarvis' head and gradually fed the liquid to the young lad.

Jarvis sighed deeply in relief.

"Thanks," he whispered.

Aaldryn slowly released him, crouching back on his heels. He motioned to Jythal.

"This is Jythal."

"Your mate?" Jarvis squinted.

Aaldryn tipped his head back and laughed.

"No, No. This is my blood-brother from my brotherhood. He is a prince."

"Oh…" Jarvis frowned. "Sorry, you all look the same."

Aaldryn waved a paw. "You will not think that when you meet Mother. She is very obviously a queen. This is our mate, Nixlye." Aaldryn unfurled his tail, allowing Nixlye to wheel forward. Jarvis' eyes shone as they scanned the young queen, assessing the difference. It was a relief, at least, that the machine within the boy was still functioning. Denvy released the tension in his shoulder muscles. Whatever had happened to the young Human had badly damaged his Human flesh, but it did seem that the philepcon liquid of the protector bot that had infected him was recovering swiftly.

Aaldryn slowly continued, his voice sturdy and comforting. "Nixlye is also a queen, but outside of this cabin she pretends to be a neutral princess. It is so that Mother is not caught out as being a prideless queen."

Nixlye inclined her head in greeting. "Your family is safe, Jarvis. The little Kelib girl refused to leave your side, so we managed to convince her to sleep in here. She was very tired."

"Probably because I gave her a little something to help with the sleep," Jythal said.

Nixlye gasped and swatted the doctor's arm. "You didn't!"

Jythal shook his head. "She knew I did. She's very good with herbs."

Tears had gathered in Jarvis' eyes, his attention upon Ki'b, sleeping in the cot by the warmth of the stove. Gradually he turned toward

Denvy. Denvy smiled. It was worth torture at the hands of Twizels—the happiness of a single child.

"Khwaja Denvy, you're all right." Jarvis clasped hands to his mouth.

Denvy approached carefully, trying not to let his aching bones and muscles reveal too much of his condition. He knelt beside the bed and reached out, brushing tears from the boy's hot cheeks. Dry skin cracked as Jarvis beamed at him. It lit Denvy's hearts with a beat of cheer, gratefulness, and relief to be alive.

"Oh, I will be, laddie. I will be. You rest now."

"But, sir, I have to go! I met the Key! And I need to—"

Denvy shook his head.

"It will be all right, Jarvis." He sent a gentle, dreamathic pulse forward, through the paw against the Human's cheek. "However important things seem right now, they will still be here on the morrow."

Jarvis' eyelids drooped, his body easing into the relief of sleep. Denvy bent forward, pressing a soft kiss to his forehead.

"You brave little soldier," he murmured.

As he rose, Denvy felt Nixlye's hand on his paw. She pulled him back to his chair, settling him down again.

"You shouldn't walk around so much. Trust me. I know all about that." Her cheeks crinkled with silent mirth.

Aaldryn clambered onto the bed, making a nest as he curled up beside Jarvis, his tail uncoiling into a thick blanket. Jythal slipped under it, his paw searching for a book that he threw at his blood-brother. "Read it to me. It's about Human anatomy."

"I thought we already knew everything about Nixlye's anatomy."

"I hear Human males are different."

"Really? Such a strange race. What's different?"

"Read it to me, and find out."

Their voices settled into the background, like the crackle of the flames in the stove that Nixlye stoked into life as she threw more compressed patties onto the coals. Denvy played his paws over the cracks in the table's wood. He felt an odd pang in his chest. Jealousy, was it? Surely not. Surely, when he looked upon the two princes, he was not jealous? Yet he had never joined a brotherhood in his youth. He had lived among Zaprexes, in their crystal fairy-castles, learning how to use his dreamathic mind, how to control machines and fly sky-ships. He had been surrounded by Zaprexes, but never truly had he been a part of their ethereal world either. He had loved them, and they had loved him—but his own people had come to fear him and he, in the end, had turned away from them because of that fear.

Denvy leant on his paw.

It was odd that he saw none of that fear now, in the two young Kattamonts nursing his hybrid cub.

They did not fear the Zaprex machine he was becoming.

Denvy stirred as a hand touched his arm and he looked at Nixlye.

"We have a legend here in Utillia about the Gold Lion who once flew the Rainbow City. It is said that the prince could make things vanish with a wave of his paw, and call them back again without a word. He had no brotherhood, no queen, he was alone…among the Angels."

Denvy raised an eyebrow.

Angels. The word was not Common Basic. It was not even Kattamont—it was Zaprex, a word from the little blue planet of his creators. How strange to hear it slipping from the lips of the beautiful young queen.

"Angels. Wherever did you hear such a word, my dear?"

She frowned. "Like I said, it is just a legend we tell. Why?"

Denvy swirled the tea-leaves in the bottom of his cup. "It is not a very Kattamont word. To hear it spoken aloud now is rather strange, that is all."

Nixlye shrugged. "Utillia is built upon the skeletons of Zaprexes. Our whole land is strange."

He chuckled. "True enough."

"You're him, aren't you, though? That Gold Lion?"

Denvy raised his brow. He let his silence be the confirmation she desired.

"Why did you never come back?"

He studied his paws. "When all you know is how to run, my dear, you simply keep running."

Small fingers touched under his chin, startling him as they lifted his head, causing him to gaze into blue Human eyes, so much like Zinkx's. "Well, you are needed here. As the Long Night comes, we will need a Gold Lion to light our way."

He had never thought it possible, in all his long sol-cycles of living, to be so counselled by one so young.

PENNY & CLIVE

CHAPTER NINE

We must not fight,
One-Before-Whom-Evil-Trembles.
We must not fight.
Not now,
When Ra has fallen beyond the horizon,
When Osiris is scattered amongst the Data,
When my Lilies whither.
Please,
How can I appease you,
My Beloved?

Private Communications Link.
Utillian Time 19:36PM.
Signal: Strong.
Upload: Completed.
Do you wish to send?

Clive's bountiful energy had returned. It was as though it had never left. Denvy chuckled, watching the boy tumbling on the large bed beside him with all the agility given to his race. Denvy startled as Penny pounced on him, wrapping a deep red scarf around his neck and tying it in an intricate knot at his chest. The sensation of the fabric against his bare neck, void of its magnificent mane, was a strange one. Penny smiled into his eyes.

"It will hide the yoke, and add some weight. Mother would wear an apron after my little brother was stillborn, she said it made her feel better. I thought…it would help you, too." Her hands were trembling as they often did whenever she mentioned her family. Like all his cubs, she, too, had her share of horrific memories and great loss.

"Thank you, my dear." Denvy touched the scarf. "Red, the colour of Messengers."

Penny hugged his large arm. "I am so glad you are all right, Khwaja Denvy."

"I am, too."

He set her down upon the floor as Clive dived into his lap, whooping loudly.

"Khwaja Denvy! You must see this place. It is so amazing! There are more Kattamonts here, just like you. I ate this disgusting thing. It was like a slug, but it was worse. Only, it tasted really nice." The boy's voice was hoarse, his neck still purple with bruises, but the swelling had improved. Denvy tipped him upside down, blowing a loud rasp into his bare stomach, which earned him a squeal in delight. He set him down, tapping him lightly on the head to send him scooting out the door.

Penny dusted off her dress, and, for the first time, Denvy took note of its little apron. Her eyes turned his way for approval and he inclined his head. Quickly she followed Clive, yelling at him to slow down. Denvy smiled faintly. Children. They had so much energy. Wearily he heaved himself off the bed. It took too much effort and it was frustrating, but with gradual ease in each step he navigated his way through the sand-ship and out onto the top deck. The wind of the morning had the briefest touch of winter, blowing across from Pennadot. It was enough to make him shiver and his fan-tail curl. The burning-sea was beginning to shine, though, and warm with the heat of the Sun. Winter would never be as harsh in Utillia, and the Long Night never as dark with the refracting crystal shine of the land.

The deck was a hive of activity, none of which he understood. He had known Zaprex vessels, and the startling chaotic rhythm that flowed on a flying machine. Folk looking upon the central control room of a lord or lady ship might have seen nothing but mayhem, but he had always experienced it as a symphony. He had been part of it. When it had been ripped from him, his life had lost its harmony—he had become a lone instrument.

It was a nice feeling, though, to be back upon the deck of a ship, even if it was not a flying machine. His foot-paws drew him to the railing, where the distinctive figure of Titus, cloaked in his rippling robe of black, stood out against the burning-sea's golden glow. The Hunter was stooped, but he straightened at his approach, throwing on his charismatic smile. Denvy felt relief. Titus did not look at his shaven mane, his sunken cheeks, and sagged skin. The Hunter knew well how demeaning a stare could be over something one could not control.

"How're yeh feeling, old man?"

"A lot better."

"Good. That is good." Titus released a pent up sigh. "Yeh had me worried, yeh know. Dying on ma watch would've been…well, none of 'em back home would've been happy about it."

Denvy leant against the rigging, watching the glossy wings of the sand-ship work against the gravity swells of the burning-sea. Further out, he caught sight of the distant tip of a Zaprex turret, glittering in the Sun's light.

"Do think yeh could get a message to ma wife?" Titus' voice was hesitant, soft, and almost child-like. Denvy's ears flipped back.

"I am sorry, Titus. The yoke still binds my dreamathic mind. My will is considerably strong, but—"

"*Tah*. It's all right." Titus gave his arm a friendly pat. "I know. I know."

They stood in silence, studying the long horizon.

Denvy shifted, his foot-paws growing weary, exhaustion filling his legs. He moved to nearby rigging, letting it take the weight off his aching limbs. "There are two dreamathics on this sand-ship. I think they might be mid-level classes."

"The white lion and the cripple?"

Denvy shook his head at the Hunter. Messengers, and their insistence on categorising people by trait rather than acknowledging the soul within. Despite Titus' own experience with hurtful labels and assumptions, it appeared it was a habit hard to break.

"Yes."

Titus rubbed his bristled chin, fingering the reddened beard beginning to grow. "Does it appear strange to yeh that, despite all the effort the House of Flames puts into breedin' dreamathics for the war, we never seem to manage anythin' higher than a minor class and yet, here in Utillia, yeh run into not just one but two mid-level classes?"

Titus looked his way. "I mean, Rein was the first high-level born in centuries. According to the records she was an abnormality. But yeh know that's not the case."

"No." Denvy breathed out wearily. "She was designed."

"Right. She was part of the first batch of the breeding program. The ones who survived, at least." Titus' voice dropped low. "You don't think…?"

"Something similar is happening here?" Denvy tucked his tail against his lap, casting his gaze back towards the Zaprex turret in the distance. "I hope not. I really hope not."

Titus' jaw tightened. Denvy himself tried to hold back the shiver that ran up his spine at memory of the horrors the Messenger's so-called 'breeding program' had produced and the subsequent campaign to bring down a corrupt government.

Zinkx had never wanted to play a part in politics, but, alas, his young ward had seemed to have a way of manoeuvring himself right into the pathway of the eldership. It was not surprising, though, considering who and what his ward truly was: the greatest secret of the Northlands, perhaps—could he claim that?

"Khwaja Denvy! Khwaja Denvy! Look. Look. Lady Zafiashid gave me a new earring!"

Denvy rubbed a paw against his ear at the sound of Clive's shrill voice. Titus' gaze softened, his lips managing a fond smile. Denvy felt a stirring of sympathy for the Hunter, whose children had been little red-haired bundles so much like Clive—and just as loud—the last time he had seen them.

Clive tore across the deck, wobbling against the uneven gravity without the grav-boots the crew wore. Denvy had a sudden vision of the little Human flying off into the burning-sea to be swept away by the rising dunes. He shook his head, clearing his mind. Surely the queen trailing after his cub had taken many measures against such a terrible thing happening.

Zafiashid's smooth movements across the deck were a testament to the sol-cycles she had spent upon the burning-sea. Her tail swayed rhythmically, keeping time with the rolling of the sand-ship. Denvy eased himself off his perch, inclining his head at her approach. Her eyes glossed over him, her jewelled gaze piercing enough to make him feel like he was a cub again, every inch of his fur being scrutinized. It did not help that her scent followed him everywhere, in all the clothing he wore, in the cabin and bed he slept in, and through the very walls of the sand-ship.

She owned every inch of the *Lawless Child*—and she let it be known.

Clive latched onto his leg, hugging it tightly. "See? Look at my new earring!"

Titus crouched down, admiring the new jewel in the collection that dangled from the boy's ear. The Hunter ruffled Clive's mop of hair. "Yer old Abbot would be proud."

Clive beamed. "That's what Lady Zafiashid said."

"Queen." Denvy corrected.

"What?" Clive cocked his head.

"The correct term of address for a female Kattamont such as Zafiashid is Queen."

Clive frowned. "Then what is Nixlye?"

"She is a princess, a neutral Kattamont who has not yet become a queen." Denvy held up his paws. "We Kattamonts have three roles we can perform. A prince, a neutral, or a queen. Princes are few, because princes are born into their role. No neutral can become a prince, but a neutral has a chance to become a princess under a queen, and, eventually, if the queen dies, they will take the place of that queen. Most Kattamonts you will come across will be neutrals or princesses."

Clive made a face and Zafiashid laughed. She gave his head a fond pat as she knelt by his side. "Be glad you are not in Sin'musk'qu, my boy. The Batitics, you will find, are more complex by far."

"I am so glad I am Human!" Clive threw his arms out dramatically, spinning on his heels. Zafiashid scooped him up, setting him on her shoulder. "You do have your advantages, even wingless." She smiled warmly.

Titus stood formally. "We thank yeh for the aid yeh've given, Queen."

Had her paw not been clamped firmly on Clive's small legs, the nonchalant shrug she gave would have rolled him off her shoulders.

"Perhaps the Rythrya Guiding Stones directed me through your path."

Titus smiled. "Paladins be honoured if that is so."

"My son tells me you are not a being of this Realm, Elemental." Zafiashid's tail flicked.

"I was just a boy, once." Titus slowly removed a glove. Denvy wrinkled his nose, smelling already the odour of burning flesh as the skin was exposed to the sunlight, peeling away until only the bones remained. He curled them together into a fist. "I'm not anymore. Like yer son, I'm the host of an Elemental. Only I took full control of the parasite. Twizels do not leave one with much choice. It is either conquer them, or be conquered."

"We are all touched in some way by the Secondary Realm's collapse." Zafiashid swung Clive and settled him upon the railing. "Some of us are just more aware of it, and bear the scars. The reminders."

She did nothing to hide the lash marks down her back, the flesh marred by whips, weapons, and claws, no longer able to grow fur to cover the wounds. Denvy rubbed his own scarred arms. He had lived centuries as an unchangeable mountain, chipped at by barely a harsh wind, and yet this young queen had more battle scars than he could ever lay claim to.

"We shall be docking at Ishabal." Zafiashid pointed towards the Zaprex turret in the distance. "It is a small trading city between Utillia and Pennadot. We must restock on Mist supplies."

Clive gaped. "If *that* is small, what happens to be big?"

Zafiashid laughed. "The Three Wind Cities are enormous, cub. They travel in a constant rotation around Utillia docking at all the little cities and islands between their routes. You have not seen the magnificence of Utillia until you have visited one of the Wind Cities."

Clive's eyes lit up with wild, excited hope. He bounced, balancing on the railing with the ease only a Human could attain. Denvy caught his arm before he could topple off, though the lad did not seem to notice how close he was to falling overboard. His pink, freckled cheeks puffed out before he erupted into a burst of loud, enthusiastic words.

"Can we go, Khwaja Denvy? Can we see the Wind Cities? Please, oh please, oh please!"

Looking across at Titus, Denvy saw the Hunter's worry, the shift of his body towards the west—toward Coltarian—the home of all Messengers. Titus' heart was not yet home. To a Messenger, duty was the burden borne until the freedom of death. The etched lines of the weariness of war carved eons into Titus' features.

"Jarvis has something he needs to tell yeh." Titus spoke over Clive's excitement. "It's important." The young Hunter turned, shifting into the safety of the shadows, away from the Sun that cursed his steps.

Denvy sighed. His ears tweaked rearwards as Zafiashid's voice spoke from behind. "I do not think it is the yoke that burdens you, old one. I think it is the weight of all the fears and worries you carry."

"You may be right about that, Queen."

Ki'b seemed in much merrier spirits, her smile brighter and the anxiety that she had been wearing like a cloak was no longer wrapped tightly around her. It was breathtaking to see the little girl dance like a child should. Leaving her, Clive, and Penny in the company of a half-breed Kelib in the galley, as stories were shared about sand-sea beasts and mighty sailors that battled them, Denvy eased his way down the corridors, tracing the dreamathic signature he had come to know as Nixlye's lavender-pink, cotton touch. He rather liked her dreamathic mind. Without the crystal visor that young Messengers wore to communicate via the dreamathic nexus, he was free to envision her mind however he desired and he pictured her as patchwork quilts, wrapped snugly about his shoulders as a comfortable, caring presence. A small, bottled-up part of him was curious, though, to know what her mind would feel like when the lioness within her lashed out without hesitation. Would the lavender-pink turn to deep white hatred and the cotton texture become piercing needles?

The door into the cabin of the little pride was unlocked and he carefully opened it, poking his head in. It was luxurious, not having to duck whenever he entered through a door. He wondered if Humans and Kelibs who dwelt in Utillia ever felt out of proportion as he had at the House of Flames or in Pennadot.

He chuckled at the amusing sight of Jarvis seated on the edge of the immense bed. Indeed, there was little doubt Humans had to feel tiny. Jarvis looked even more a child in the large cabin, designed for the stature of Aaldryn and Jythal.

Jarvis looked up, grinning.

"Khwaja Denvy, sir!" He slipped off the bed, landing on bare feet, and rushed to him. Denvy breathed out as the young lad bumped up against his midriff, hugging him tightly.

"You are looking much better, Jarvis."

Colour had returned to the young Wynnila's cheeks, though it was a flush of blue and not the usual red of Human blood. It made for a strange ferrous tone to his skin's hue, even in the light of the lanterns and candles. Jarvis rubbed the back of his neck sheepishly. "Thanks."

He stepped back, allowing entrance and Denvy eased inside, closing the door behind him. Titus lounged in a chair at the table, sipping on a large flagon of what smelt like fine beer. Denvy brushed at his nose. Typical of the hunter; they made dock at a port and the first thing the Messenger did was buy a cask of alcohol. Jythal was seated beside him, his laughter rich with crinkled lines of cheer written across his features as he listened with erect ears to the wild tales of the Hunter.

"Master Titus has been going on about the Battle of Phebes for a while."

"Ah." Denvy puffed out his chest. "One of Zinkx's greatest moments."

"Is it true he killed a High Class Twizel?" Jarvis piped up. "Or is it just a story?"

Denvy raised his eyebrows and placed a paw gently on Jarvis' shoulder, leading him towards the merriment in the kitchen corner of the cabin. "It is honestly not my tale to tell."

Jarvis pouted.

"Though I do hear you have quite an interesting story yourself."

A mechanical glow brightened behind Jarvis' eyes as a soft pattern of light played gently down the skin of his cheeks. He hopped onto a large seat beside Titus, reaching for one of the enormous mugs on the table. "It was amazing, Khwaja Denvy."

Jarvis pulled the heavy flagon closer, sloshing the honey-dew within. Nixlye rolled over and passed Jarvis a smaller tankard.

"Here, I think this one might be easier for you to use. This is one of mine. Bit smaller."

"Thanks." Jarvis gratefully accepted it, eagerly sipping the sweet liquid. Denvy watched the boy's bare toes curl in glee. He shook his head. Titus was a terrible influence already. At least it was only honey-dew in Jarvis' mug. He glanced gratefully at Nixlye, who inclined her head.

Aaldryn placed savoury muffins, fresh from the stove, on the table and swung himself over a chair, grabbing the flagon Jarvis had discarded. "Thanks for the drink, Titus."

"Ah, least I could do to thank yeh." Titus held up his beverage in a toast.

"Haven't had good beer in sol-cycles. Never enough coin for the clean stuff." Aaldryn responded.

The two clinked their flagons together. Jythal grabbed a muffin before they were caught in the crossfire of sloshing liquid.

"It'll be a long night now," the blind doctor muttered.

"Well, they are getting longer." Jarvis quipped.

"But worse with drunkards." Jythal buttered his muffin. "So, I believe we have gathered for a purpose this evening?"

"*Tah*, always straight to the point, brother. Never any merriment with you." Aaldryn pouted and leant heavily on Jythal's arm, a loud purr emanating from his chest.

Denvy frowned. "Should we not wait for Queen Zafiashid?"

"Mother is not permitted in this cabin." Aaldryn's air-gills spiked slightly as he breathed out. "Don't worry. She banned herself. She does not like to be reminded of her loss of pride status. We'll fill her in later."

"She trusts you that much with the affairs of this sand-ship?" It was impossible to hide the surprise in his voice, but Denvy could not stop himself from looking at Nixlye. She reached out, giving his paw a pat.

"We're a family. We trust each other."

"I can understand that," Titus said.

"I figured a Messenger would." Nixlye leant her arms on the table. "Is it beautiful? The House of Flames?"

"More than yeh can imagine. But I grew up there, so I am a little biased." Titus waved a hand. "In truth, Coltarian is a stunning land. Sure it tries its best to kill yeh every day, but it has its own unique beauty." His gaze drew distant. "We like to say that the House of Flames isn't so much a place—it's the ideals, the values, the strength each Messenger carries wherever they go that make them the House of Flames no matter where they are. We all bleed red."

Titus exhaled, shaking himself slightly. He fiddled in his jacket pocket, tugging out the folded piece of parchment discovered in the Zaprex Way Station on the edge of the Ovin-tu Mountains. Denvy's heart raced, his mind thrown back to the last moment he had seen Zinkx, vanishing into the darkness of a Pennadotian forest on the back of a diabond, a Kelib woman tucked behind him, her eyes wide with fear. The note was the only thing he had to cling to the hope Zinkx was still alive.

A note scrawled with the foretelling of the coming kismet of the Northlands.

Titus passed it to Nixlye, as though it were naught but another missive, and not the guide he treasured. "This is why we're here, passing through Utillia."

Slowly Nixlye's brow creased in a frown. Had she air-gills they would likely have begun to halo her head in a rise of concern, but, instead, a loud purr rose from her chest. Both Jythal and Aaldryn sat straighter in their chairs, their fur stiffening in reaction to their queen's unease. She finally breathed out and read aloud.

"To all Messengers of Pennadot,

This is High Commander Zinkx Maz. Be warned: Coltarian is to erupt come the High Summer Solstice. Head as far North as you can. Take as many Pennadotians with you as possible. Seek refuge in Utillia. Get word to the House—the Key has been found, the Dragon is rising. The Age of the Black Sun has begun.

Your Brother,
Zinkx Maz"

Nixlye settled her hands into her lap, staring down at the worn parchment on the table. Slowly she looked at Aaldryn. "As archaeologists we've always known about the Dragon. It is hard not to believe in something when every text you uncover in the sunken ruins refers to the Thousand Sol-Cycle Wars."

"And Khamsin's stories are terrifying," Jythal muttered.

"But Coltarian erupting?" Nixlye squeezed her eyes shut, rubbing thumb and finger against the bridge of her nose. "Is that even possible?"

"It has always been a possibility," Khamsin's voice, so slightly lower than Aaldryn's, interjected.

Denvy tensed at the intrusion of the Elemental Titan. The cabin's air-pressure had shifted, just enough to feel tight against his skin.

"That is why the Zaprexes created the Obelisk System, so that my sibling would be chained nice and tightly to her little rock."

"That's just it." Titus lifted a hand. "If Coltarian is going to erupt, why wouldn't Prometheus have said something earlier? Surely she'd ha' known the Obelisk System was going offline?" The Hunter massaged his temples. "She'd ha' said something and started the evacuation—"

Khamsin snorted. "You are giving my sibling far too much credit. It has been a long time since the Zaprexes strapped her down. Mayhap she is tired of being contained."

The Hunter bent forward, glaring at the Titan within the young Kattamont prince. "That doesn't sound like the Prometheus I know. The Elemental who raised me loved all things, abundantly. She'd never willingly destroy the Northlands."

Khamsin shrugged awkwardly. "We are Titans. We existed before the Zaprexes came here."

Jarvis lifted his head suddenly, his voice eerily monotone. "Yes, but the Zaprexes gave you consciousness. You owe them that."

Khamsin laughed heartily. "True enough, little Changeling. True enough."

"This Key, though—" Nixlye's glare settled Khamsin's laughter. "I think it is mentioned in a few of the later records, but those tend to get very sketchy on details."

"That is not surprising." Denvy shifted forward on his seat, resting his paws on the table. "After the Cataclysm of Kemet, the Zaprexes sank the last of their cities, and the few who did remain survived here in Utillia trying to devise a plan to save Livila." He cleared his throat, emotion threatening to choke his words. "It is those few Zaprexes we must thank today for our lives. They are the ones who make mention of the Key. For the Key was likely their hope as well."

Jythal leant forward. "And what is it?"

"Ah, the Key." Khamsin turned stiffly to face him. "The Key was apparently a legendary Zaprex device, perhaps a weapon created in the last hope to end the Sol-Cycle Wars, or an escape off this rock they tried to call home."

"The Creators wouldn't leave!" Jarvis snapped.

"Some say it was a guide to the lost Towers," Khamsin continued, ignoring Jarvis' outburst.

"Is this Zinkx Maz a good source? Can he be relied upon?" Nixlye stared down at the parchment.

"Zinkx is—*was*—my ward," Denvy said slowly. "And the High Commander of the Blood Armada. He can always be relied upon."

"Then we should stock up on Mist supplies." Jythal scratched his chin. "Mist is about to become very, very pricy."

Titus frowned. "Is that all yeh care about?"

"Think about it: if Pennadot falls our main source of water is gone. We barely make it with our Mist Farms now. You increase our population with refugees from Pennadot and we are going to have a problem sustaining ourselves." Jythal shrugged. "Just saying. Tomorrow I think we should stock up."

"Mother will agree." Nixlye massaged her temples. "We are on the verge of change. The Era of the Black Sun. I like that." She glanced briefly out the small window. "It gives hope despite the darkness."

"There is always hope." Denvy cut open another muffin.

"Yes, there is. Which is why what Jarvis has to say is rather interesting." Titus raised his hand. "Jarvis, how about yeh tell everyone what happened in the Zaprex flying machine." The Hunter accepted the torn note back from Nixlye, returning it to his shirt pocket.

Jarvis worried his hands anxiously in his lap for a few moments before breathing in deeply. His brow furrowed in concentration. "The Zaprex ship's name was *Bez-at:_Who_Lingers_by_Water:* a warhawk class. When the Twizel attacked us, I was accidently thrown against one of its terminals, and I logged into the warhawk's computers." Jarvis frowned. "You have to understand—*Bez-at:_Who_Lingers_by_Water,* its Matrix Crystal had grown out of containment, so it had no way to control its firewalls. I was cast into the Secondary Realm, and—"

His shoulders curled. Nixlye reached out, laying a hand gently on one of his legs. Was she feeling something Denvy could no longer sense due to the yoke around his neck? The emotions the boy was radiating: fear? Was Jarvis afraid? His body was quivering in an uncontrolled manner and Denvy squeezed his paws tightly, horrified that he had missed it. He cursed himself inwardly for his continued reliance on his dreamathic mind. Had the box not taught him anything? To function with the yoke binding him, he needed to learn to read without his dreamathic skills. He needed to see with real eyes again, not those of a program.

"The Dragon was there." Jarvis finished in a breathless whisper.

"You met the Dragon?" Denvy croaked out.

"Yes." Jarvis' eyes turned his way. Large, wide, white disks they had become, glowing with a backlight. "He tried to take over my mind.

And, sir...I think he would have, if it hadn't been for the Key."

A smile suddenly lit up Jarvis features, changing the emotion in the cabin with a single sweep. It was as though the protector bot within the boy had released a pulse of pure, happy bliss that burst in a bubble. "Oh, Khwaja Denvy, it was so amazing to meet a real Zaprex!" Jarvis clutched his hands to his swelling chest, his cheeks glowing with radiant glee.

"He called himself Semyueru, or just Sam, and he was the most beautiful thing I've ever seen."

"Semyueru?" Denvy rubbed his chin.

Jarvis nodded. He carefully pulled off the necklace around his neck, the one he never removed. He passed it over and Denvy cradled the small glass prism in the palm of his paw. The delicate piece of glass was so tiny, but so much Zaprex technology had been, even when he had been a young cub.

"The Key said I needed to take this crystal to the House of Flames and meet him there. It is part of a Map. A Map to the Towers."

"Holy Sun on High." Titus bellowed a laugh. "Zinkx did it!" The Hunter grabbed at his arm and Denvy felt himself shaken. "The good ol' Commander actually did it. He found what the Dreamers who Dreamt spoke about! Oh, think of what ma wife is gonna say! No one believed them, Denvy—no one but us!" Titus pumped a fist in the air. "Tha's right, yeh stinking High Elder! Once again, Squad Sixteen wins the bet!"

Denvy closed his eyes, wrapping his paw around the small, precious prism. A tiny sliver of technology—a tiny piece of hope. Did he dare believe it? That the Key was truly a Zaprex reborn in this era? The crystal grew warm against his skin, the nano-bots within his body flooding toward it, trying to activate it and he chuckled at the sensation of heat. Carefully he returned it to Jarvis, despite the pull against relinquishing it.

"Do you see, sir? I was given a task by the Key." Jarvis clutched the prism to his chest. "I have to fulfil it. I have to go to the House of Flames and meet him."

How Denvy wished the growing weight in his stomach would leave. Zinkx had been about Jarvis' age when he had commanded the Battle of Phebes and taken on the burden of the task that had shaped his future. He only wished he could protect every last one of his children—

I have far too much Zaprex in me, Denvy mused silently. *I have come full circle. I am my Creators. I want to protect everyone.*

"So it seems, then," Nixlye drummed her fingers on the armrests of her wheelchair, "that you need to get to Coltarian. I guess you have planned to cut across Utillia?"

Titus nodded. "Is it possible to get a small sand-ship or something?"

"It is possible." Nixlye clicked her tongue. "But in the Long Night...I don't know if you'll make the crossing."

Titus slumped in his chair, muttering foul language.

Denvy reached out a comforting paw, clasping the Hunter's knee. "I suppose now that I am well enough—"

Titus cut him off, "Oh, no, no, yeh're staying here! Something is going on in Utillia. We know it. And when Coltarian erupts, old man, yeh're gonna be needed here. I'll keep going."

"But it is unlikely that the Eldership will believe anything written by Zinkx now," Denvy rebutted, and watched Titus' cheeks flush with righteous anger.

"Titus, you know very well that Zinkx was already on bad soil with the Eldership when we left. He would have been branded a traitor by now."

"*Tah*, the *jraki* pieces of *chari*! The lot of 'em!"

"So they won't believe us?" Jarvis looked pained. "About any of it?"

Denvy sighed. It was terribly complicated, the child-run government of the Messengers. He had never felt comfortable amongst them—always they had seemed like toddlers, trying to be the loudest in the room. "The only ones loyal to us are old members of the Sixteenth Squad. It is likely, in the current political climate, you'd have the Medical Guild, the Agricultural Guild, and the Mechanical Guild on your side."

"Yah," Titus scoffed. "All guilds connected to the Thyrrhos Nation." Titus dipped his head wearily, speaking as though he was trying convince himself. "Raphael is pretty convincing. She's the High Medic," he explained to Jarvis, "and the Soul of Prometheus. Her position is very high ranking. She could possibly pull off a *coup d'état*."

"That sounds a bit drastic." Jythal scratched behind an ear.

Titus shrugged. "You do not know the Eldership."

Denvy pinched the bridge of his nose. "We do not want to start civil war inside the House of Flames, Titus. I realize you might feel one is building between the Thyrrhos and the Soldiers' Guild, but we hardly need to add fuel to the fire by forcing Raphael's hand."

"What if we have to?" Jarvis piped up. "What if the only way to get everyone to evacuate is to do something drastic?"

Denvy shook his head. "Lad, I want you to listen very carefully. Use battle as your very last choice; use words as your first option. If you can talk to your enemy, talk first. You never know what they might say."

Titus snorted. "Pacifist hogwash."

Khamsin held up Aaldryn's paws. "By the sound of it, you have the Soul of Prometheus with you. That means you have the Thyrrhos Nation behind you. That, I say, is enough of a reason to go."

Jarvis looked hopeful again. Denvy did not dare crush the boy's will with negativity. The lad could not understand what it meant to be a Soul of an Elemental, nor one as powerful a Titan as Prometheus, but it was plain to see the young warrior was storing the information.

"Guess that means I'm heading off." Titus scrubbed a hand through his hair.

"And me too!" Jarvis' wrapped a hand tightly around the small prism. "I promised the Key."

Aaldryn's paw settled over Nixlye's hand, squeezing it tightly, the natural movement providing a clue that the Kattamont was back in charge of his body. "They'll need someone to guide them. If Khamsin and I go, we can cut down the time drastically. They won't need to rely entirely on Mist, either."

Nixlye's lips narrowed. Her purring heightened to a soft whine. "I know."

"Khamsin," Aaldryn lowered his head onto her arm, "truly wishes to reconcile with his sibling. If Prometheus is alive, I have to go."

Nixlye brushed back his air-gills from his ears, gently pressing a soft kiss to his forehead.

"No." Jarvis stood. "You need to stay here. You shouldn't be leaving your Pride, Aaldryn. We'll be fine."

Aaldryn's tail lazily looped about, coming to rest over Jythal's shoulders.

"This is why we form brotherhoods. Jythal will take over while I am gone. Everyone will be fine. We all have our duties; some quests take us from those we love."

No truer words had come from a prince so young. Denvy lifted his flagon to his lips, letting the liquid linger down his throat. He had spent his centuries running from the duty of his past.

Had it finally caught up with him? He had left behind all those he had loved here in the land of burning sand and, somewhere, their corpses still lay below the golden ocean, waiting for his return.

I'm sorry. I'm sorry. I was too late. But I've come back. I'll stay this time. I promise.

His drink did not taste as sweet as he wished it did, but he toasted silently to the lost souls of a war long ago.

Ki'b lay beside Jarvis, curled up tightly in the bed that swamped both of them in a mountain of pillows and blankets. They smelt so inviting, filled with the aromas he had come to realise were Jythal, Aaldryn, and Nixlye's scents. He tangled a hand through Ki'b's short locks of hair. They were finally becoming smooth and sleek, no longer so coarse due to being shaven off. She would grow to be a beautiful Kelib woman.

Already he could see it. Her hair would be long again, flowing in the wind, and she would wear the proudest of grins, a brash smirk, like she knew something he did not. All he had known of her before the light of the world had revealed her to him had been her sweet little voice in the darkness, and brief glimpses of her humble, pale eyes. Had she not told him she was Kelib, he would never have known. Darkness made all equal. The Long Night would make them all equal again. He bent, despite the ache still grating in his chest, and pressed a soft kiss to her forehead.

Leaving her, and Clive and Penny, when they had promised to be a family forever—was he breaking a bond he was not supposed to break? He had sworn he would protect them. He was the eldest, and the eldest brother was supposed to look after his siblings—was that not Pennadotian tradition?

The ache he had thought was the wound biting at his iron began to creep gradually up his throat, until he felt the burning of tears escape his eyes. He covered his mouth, holding back the sobs.

The floor of the cabin creaked, startling him, and Jarvis turned his head sharply.

He saw the lethal shape of Jythal in the light of the dim lantern beside him. The white Kattamont knelt by the bed, holding out a handkerchief, and Jarvis took it, wiping snot from his nose.

"Nixlye and I will take good care of her," Jythal whispered.

"I know," Jarvis mumbled. "I just wish I could be in two places at once."

Jythal eased himself up and slipped in under the covers. His warmth filled the sheets with an overwhelming extra layer of security as his fan-tail folded over them. Ki'b rolled, pressing closer to Nixlye's slumbering shape. Jarvis watched as the queen's own tail lazily flapped about briefly before she too calmed. He settled back against Jythal's arm. The Kattamont smelt like the herbs he mixed, and the tea he liked to serve.

"You have a difficult road ahead of you, Jarvis. Don't make it harder by wishing for impossible things." Jythal's chest vibrated in a deep rumble. "We are the Misfit Pride. We do not really belong anywhere anymore. So Ki'b will be safe with us. Nixlye knows how to care for a princess like Ki'b who has been cast aside by her own people."

"She'll be a princess?" Jarvis looked up at the blind prince.

"Of course. You are a prince."

"But I'm not a Kattamont."

"That is not the point of the Misfit Pride. We accept all."

Jarvis felt him shift and he was pressed deeper into the prince's arm and chest. "You are a part of the brotherhood now. I will do my best as your brother to watch over your family. We Kattamonts protect our own."

Jarvis squeezed his eyes shut as the tears snaked down his cheeks. He let his tense body relax slowly against Jythal's stronger, sturdier form and he curled his hands between the feathers of his fan-tail. Here he had found a family, unafraid of the machine growing inside him.

Only he was so suddenly being forced to leave again.

Duty, responsibility—or family?

Which was truly more important?

He opened his eyes, staring out of the small window across the cabin.

Perhaps he was asking the wrong question entirely.

QUEEN ZAFIASHID OF THE MISFIT PRIDE
OUTCAST OF THE SLIVERTIDE PRIDE

CHAPTER TEN

01010011 01100101 01101110
01100100 00100000 01000010
01100101 01100101 01110010

NORTHERN TOWER – PRIVATE COMMUNICATION LINKAGE –
01010011 01100101 01101011 01101000 01101101 01100101 01110100

Jarvis shivered under the winter coat borrowed from Nixlye's collection. It was not the chill of the morning air, sneaking up under his clothes, but the overwhelming influx of information regarding the new surrounds that brought on the quivering. The touch of the wind and the tiny particles glossing against his skin painted the world around him more thoroughly than the roar from the bustling harbour he could barely tune out. He opened his eyes. The mechanical lenses adjusted to the brilliant desert light in soft flickers, pixels shifting to realign themselves as colours recalibrated. Jarvis clicked his tongue. The visual view screen of his optical display took in the world at an alarming rate, and his Human mind still struggled to process the information. It made his spine ache from the overload of sensory data travelling through the nerves. Hopefully it would pass in time. The headaches were frustrating.

He shook his head, trying to clear the little red warning light from one side of his lens. It sat there constantly, an irritating little blip, a visual itch he could not get rid of. Whatever had the Key meant when it said the sector he was in was destabilizing? Had they not moved away from the sector where *Bez-at:_Who_Lingers_by_Water* was? Thus far every scan he ran came up with nothing to show. He blew back his fringe and cast his gaze towards the arches of the Zaprex turret, lording over the small trading city of Ishabal. The interlinking metal and glass structures should have made him feel safe, but somehow the cobbled-together city, built up on stilts like a skirt around the ankles of the turret, radiated the deepest sensation of dread. He was standing on little but dry, splintered wood and beaten iron brought up from the depths of the burning-sea, pieced together with nothing but mud and ropes.

"Yeh all right there, Sonny Jon?" Titus called.

He had lingered too long in one place and must have stilled into a statue. He hated to cause his master to worry.

"I'm fine, sir." Jarvis bounced over loose planks, quickly catching up with the Hunter and Aaldryn. They were waiting by the holding area of cargo crates far larger than any he had ever seen. Jarvis ran his sensitive fingers briefly over one. It held live trade, possibly cows, imported from Pennadot, and he wondered where they would be heading. It appeared they were going to be loaded on a nearby sand-ship so enormous it dwarfed the *Lawless Child* several times over.

"How are we supposed to find a little boat?" He looked hopefully at Aaldryn, who swept his gaze over the harbour.

"You'd be surprised what you can find here at Ishabal. Pretty much everything can be bought and sold. Ishabal is a fair-trade city." Aaldryn chuckled at his blank stare. "It means it isn't run by the Iposti State. It's a city for outcasts, pirates, and folk who evade the taxation laws."

Titus frowned. "Why don' it get shut down then?"

Aaldryn shrugged and began to trot down a flight of stairs, towards the dock managers' stations in the distance. "The Iposti might own the burning-sea but someday we will take it back."

"Plotting to take down a government." Titus rubbed his hands together. "I like it."

Aaldryn laughed. "Figured you would."

Jarvis gripped the railings of the rickety stairs in a vice. The wind fluttered his hair. Was it the same wind swirling over his father's farmland, that had chased him as a child running free in the long Pennadotian grass? He smiled, releasing his hands and brushing them against his tunic. This was true freedom—freedom to choose his own path. The wind's freedom.

The *Lawless Child* bobbed on the burning-sea as though it were a dainty little leaf caught on the surface of a pond. Sitting in a lively harbour, surrounded by trading sand-ships that loomed over the small nyhot, it made for a rather pretty sight. The immense trading sand-ships were shambled together barrels, metal caskets with cracked hulls appearing ancient and worn by their lives upon the burning-sea. While their wings and sails were currently wrapped tightly, when released the sight would be majestic, like the train of a fine frock around a lady's ankles. Denvy almost wished he could behold the old lugging vessels leaving the harbour, just to catch a glimpse of their sails. Now he understood Jythal's concern the night before over the drop in Mist supplies. The fuel that ran the engines of the magnificent sand-ships, and, no doubt, much of technology the Kattamont race had built, surrounded him everywhere in the port, strapped to the Kattamonts who strolled past so casually, and to the Humans and Kelibs who scurried around them. Contraptions for deep burning-sea diving, cranes for hoisting cargo into the trading vessels, small floating trolleys whizzing around, but most disturbing were the pistols and the blades, all Mist operated, all alarming to behold.

Denvy dipped away from the paw that came up swiftly, patting his cheek. He hissed, slapping the touch aside.

Zafiashid's rich laughter followed as she twirled around him, skipping over the loose planks of the harbour on her dainty foot-paws.

"You are far too tense, even for an old warrior."

"I have learnt the moment I relax my guard, something awful tends to jump out."

"Me? Awful?" She gave her chest a pat, causing her fur and air-gills to fluff out in a show of her beautiful colours. Denvy huffed. Her paw latched onto his arm, pulling him along.

"Now, now, you need to enjoy yourself."

"This world is too foreign to me," he grumbled. "And what are these strange things?" He picked at the pistol hanging from the belt around her waist, holding down the pleats of her loose kilt. "Weapons? Do you trade them with the Humans of Pennadot?"

Zafiashid scoffed. "Rythrya, no! Mist manufacturing and all its wonders is entirely Utillian." She glanced at the sky-sea. "I don't entirely understand the process but I don't believe it's possible to produce Mist in Pennadot, nor do I think it works beyond the Border."

Denvy rubbed his chin. "Interesting."

The queen smiled. "Are you worried about your precious little Pennadotians?"

"I worry about everything," Denvy grumbled. "I am incapable of not worrying."

"*Tah.*" She danced around him once more, this time shifting onto all fours, rubbing against his legs before clambering up a tower of crates and perching lazily over the edge. "You must learn to live in the present, in the now, not when, then, and over there."

He raised an eyebrow. "And how did you learn this?"

She smirked, arching her back. "It's a process."

Turning away from the queen lounging across the crates, Denvy surveyed the passing crew. None paid any attention to their captain as she tapped her thick bladed claws on the side of the supplies. They all wore the same weapons as the queen, though. It did make it easier to spot which scurrying burning-seafolk belonged to the *Lawless Child*.

"Are you expecting trouble?" he queried.

Zafiashid slapped her paw down against the pistol at her side. "Just a bit of insurance."

She uncoiled herself and landed beside him.

"Insurance?" Denvy scoffed. "I thought that is what *this* is for." He swung his fan-tail, waving it in front of her nose. She brushed it aside with a barking laugh.

"Not here, you old man. This is Ishabal! This is not some outland island or a fight-pit." She shoved something cold into his paw and he froze at its familiar texture. "I do believe this is yours." Her paw gave his cheek another fond pat. This time he managed to repress the hiss as she rubbed his scent-glands.

"Do try not to get into too much trouble." She swaggered off, her voice bellowing out over the dock as she waved to a neutral Kattamont in the distance. Denvy stared down at the object in his grasp with a fond smile. The hilt of his water-sword glittered, and, as if his muscles were reminded of battle days, they tightened around it. Denvy scrubbed at his air-gills, shaking his head. He hooked the hilt to his belt, looking at Zafiashid, lording over the neutral who stood atop a crate in an attempt to better the queen.

What was it going to take for him to figure the exiled queen out?

The neutral she was yelling at seemed to have enough bite to not take Zafiashid's gusto to heart. Denvy shifted slightly as Jythal's scent caught his attention. The prince was startlingly silent in his approach and Denvy cocked his head to watch the blind Kattamont wander between crates and crew-folk, bearing a large parasol to shade himself from the Sun. Though Kattamonts wore very little Human clothing, it seemed as though Nixlye's love of her Human culture had managed to affect her mates and they proudly wore homespun scarves and large ponchos for winter. They at least added some colour to Jythal's pale tones.

"Is Mother giving poor Kuhrl a hard time again?"

"Kuhrl?" That had to be the neutral the exiled queen was dressing down.

"Kuhrl is the Mist Expeditor. Usually Aaldryn deals with the Mist supplies. Mother is…ah…not very tactful." Jythal laughed softly. "I don't think they teach queens like Mother how to speak to neutrals."

Denvy sighed. "Something we'll have to work on."

Jythal gave his arm a pat, though Denvy had a feeling he had been aiming for his shoulder. "Have fun with that. If you would excuse me. I'm going to go and interrupt before Mother blows our chances of ever buying a triple supply of Mist." Jythal's head turned towards the Sun and he wrinkled his nose in disgust. "I tend not to come out unless I have to. Ah, by the way, if you are looking for your cubs, they are with Nixlye." Jythal pointed down the harbour. "Over there by the opening to the markets, with the street urchins. Nixlye likes to sell her wares when we get here, but before that she hands out supplies to the misfit-born at Mother's wish."

Jythal twirled his parasol. The crew parted way for him. They appeared utterly relieved to see him moving towards Zafiashid. Denvy ruffled his air-gills in amusement as he started in the ambiguous direction Jythal had pointed. For a vague moment he wondered how the blind prince had known where his mate was, before he, too, picked up on the faint dreamathic colour of Nixlye's mind. As he pushed through the milling morning crowd of burning-seafolk, harbour workers, and market sellers, he kept tight his surprise at not being stopped for his odd pelt tone. Nixlye had presented him with a heavy, woven poncho, something many of the Kattamonts around him wore to shield them from the chilled winter air. He had not expected to blend in so easily.

He heard the laughter of children before he reached the wrought iron gates of the market. They arched between two smaller spires of the Zaprex turret, bent and twisted into place. Kattamont guards stood either side, watching in silent amusement as a group of grubby children surrounded Nixlye's wheelchair. Perched on Nixlye's lap sat Clive with a large cloth bag. He handed out torn off pieces of freshly baked bread to the children. The smile on Clive's face was brilliant to behold. The lad had even put on what looked like a handmade cap, resembling what he would have worn as a trainee monk at the Temple from where he had hailed.

Denvy whistled and all heads turned his way. The younger cubs clambered for him, surrounding his ankles. He heard Nixlye's laughter. "Oh, you've done it now. They'll never let you go. They like princes."

His heart ached. How he wished his dreamathic mind was healed, that the yoke did not bind him, so he could dream for the sweet faces surrounded him new clothing, healthy food, and fresh buckets of water, and fill their thin stomachs with something more than the bread Nixlye and Clive handed them.

"*Tah, tah* children. Get off the weak, skinny prince. He is nothing but bones. You will break him."

Denvy heard himself hiss again as Zafiashid's paw slid over his shoulder, her silken fur sliding smoothly against his own as she slunk past, sweeping through the horde of children, spreading them in a wave.

"You did not harm poor Kuhrl, did you Mother?" Nixlye hefted Clive off her lap, setting him down beside Penny.

Zafiashid rolled her eyes. "Jythal decided to take over the bartering. He said I am too blunt. You should speak to your prince about respecting a queen."

"He does respect you, Mother. That is why he wanted to make sure you didn't kill Kuhrl."

"Hah!" Zafiashid scoffed, grabbing the bag of bread from Clive. "Like I would do such a distasteful thing."

Nixlye eyed the queen. "Need I remind you of—"

"Don't speak of it." Zafiashid knelt and began to hand out more bread, her harsh features softening. Denvy pursed his lips, crossing his arms as he tapped a paw on the wooden planks beneath him. Zafiashid threw him a thin smile.

"You are surrounded by children once again. It seems, for an old warrior, you cannot escape them."

Denvy ruffled what was left of his beard. "Ah, yes, well, cubs are the bane of my existence. I have lived a long time but never fathered any, so I always do seem to gravitate to the children of the world."

She ducked her head. "Am I young to you, then?"

"A mere youth, my dear." The jeer leaving his mouth was an utter surprise. He had never acted so childishly. However the retort was out before he could stop it. Swiftly he turned before anything else decided to burst forth, and he followed Nixlye through the wide gates of the market.

"And you are still a sack of bones!" He heard Zafiashid's shouted remark and glanced back, catching sight of her sitting amongst the street urchins, all hungrily eating their pieces of bread. The sight tugged his chest. An exiled queen, surrounded by children, forgotten by society. He wished he could have frozen the image in time, or used one of the old Zaprex memory-capturers. His foot-paws carried him away from her, following after his cubs as they trotted beside Nixlye and her wheelchair.

Penny gripped his paw, looking anxiously at the foreign surrounds. "Should we just leave Queen Zafiashid like that?" she piped up.

"Don't worry." Nixlye thrust against the wheels of her chair. "Mother doesn't like being out of sight of the *Lawless Child* for long, and she enjoys helping the street urchins. She rather feels they are like her."

"They were so dirty," Penny griped.

Clive looked at her with a frown. "And that was a problem, because?"

"Well…I just…why couldn't they wash?"

"Mist costs a lot, and water a lot more." Nixlye shook her head. "Even this close to the Border with Pennadot. The street urchins have to rely on the weekly handouts from the Mist Expeditor. Washing is not really a high priority. Kattamonts can last longer without drinking, so the older Kattamonts tend to water the Humans and Kelibs first. That is why you'll notice the older Kattamonts look worse off."

"Oh…" Penny touched the pouch strapped to her side under her apron. "I wish I had given them my water, then.

Clive shrugged at Penny. "It's like Monk work—we would do this all the time when I was at the Temple. The Hundred Sol-Cycle Trading Collapse caused a lot of families to be displaced, to lose their farms, their homes. Many refugees would come through the Temple, too."

Penny looked down, scrubbing her shoes against the wooden planks. "Tempath was not affected by the Trading Collapse."

With more maturity than he usually displayed, Clive gave her a hug. "Isn't that a good thing? You should be happy your home wasn't hurt like the rest of Pennadot."

"But I was hurt," Penny whispered. "My family was hurt."

"We're your family now." Ki'b took Penny's hand, pulling her gently. "Come on. I'm sure Khwaja Denvy will buy you something beautiful! Won't you, Khwaja Denvy?"

Denvy felt around anxiously for a moment, thinking about the large pouch of rubies Titus had left him earlier that morning. He relaxed when he felt it still attached to his hip-bags.

"Of course, my dears."

He could not save every child in Livila, but at least he could spoil those in front of him, and love them as dearly as his old hearts could manage.

The shops and houses of the city around them were built in levels above the burning-sea, upon stilts and up against the sides of the looming Zaprex turret. The Kattamonts looked foreign to him. With their mismatched technology attached to limbs and air-gills, some with whole tails removed and replaced with wobbling, rusty mechanical pipes for balance. They matched the world they had built, an environment of pieced-together shambles of aged wood, petrified by time, dragged up from the ruins of the long-buried forests below the sands, and Zaprex metal scavenged and butchered.

Penny and Ki'b had taken off into the crowd, heading toward a jewellery bazaar. He could trust that was where they would stay. Both had an adoration of jewellery and coming into Utillia had only fuelled their love of piercings and necklaces. It was, at least, something the two girls had in common.

Clive gave a boyish snort. "What is it with them and rocks?"

"I believe Ki'b is looking for some stones to make her Kelib necklace," Nixlye said gently.

"And do remember, Clive, Penny is from Tempath. Her father was a miner; she knows all about stones."

Clive pulled a face. Nixlye reached out, pinching his cheeks. "Careful, the wind will change and you'll end up stuck with an ugly face. Come along. I think I know what you'll like."

"How do you know what I like?" Clive blew a rasp.

"You seem like rather a smart lad to me. You must have read a lot of books and scrolls in that Temple of yours."

"Oh, yes!" Clive puffed out his chest. "The Monks said I was made to be a scholar, because my Papa was a bard! I have the gift for it."

Nixlye, it seemed, knew just how to flatter Clive into peace. She soon had the boy beaming, and he bounced along, telling them of all the incredible things he had read as Nixlye directed them across the street. Denvy kept Ki'b and Penny in sight, through the shifting bodies, and Nixlye rolled herself up to what he thought at first was a blacksmith. It was the second glance that caught him off guard, drawing his attention to the array of mechanical goods scattered over the desks and hanging on the walls of the small stall. Beyond was a dwelling built up a wall of the Zaprex turret. A Human man sat behind the desk, working silently on a greasy piece of metal. It shone a soft, purple sheen. Denvy's stomach twisted.

It was Zaprex metal, pure and beautiful, untouched by the rust of time. How deep, he wondered, had they needed to travel below the surface of the burning-sea to find such a treasure? How expensive was the metal that had belonged to the fairy race?

Nixlye thumped her fist down on the desk. "Rythrya's blessings, Obakjen!"

"Why lookie what the Northern Wind has brought us. If it isn't the rosy beauty Nixlye. How fair you today?" The Human could not have been older than forty sol-cycles, but the Utillian air had not been kind to him, and Denvy could smell the odour of disease and decay emanating from the man.

He rose stiffly to his feet, his smile handsome over tattooed cheeks beautifully inked with colours as though he was mimicking a Kattamont's air-gills.

"I am well, Obakjen." Nixlye fished out a bag from beneath a knitted blanket. "I finished your order. I hope it is to your liking."

"Thank you, dear."

"Aaldryn provided the feathers for the trim. He's been shedding a lot lately. He hopes you approve."

"As usual, it is beautiful. Please do tell Prince Aaldryn that his colours are still as impressive as the day he tried to lop off my head. Finally, something to keep my weary old legs warm this winter."

Clive peered over the edge of the bench. "What is all this stuff?"

The Human vendor spread his hands wide, grinning down at him. "It's all stuff brought up from the below the burning-sea, lad. My son—Where is he? Just a minute—" Obakjen turned and shouted, "Ryojin, get down here! Nixlye's visiting!"

A head appeared through a small window, air-gills of yellows and pale blues fluttering with excitement. "Nixlye! I'll be right down."

Denvy winced as the house shuddered. He had a horrible vision of the whole shack coming down around them, but it held, and out through the curtain of a small door burst a prince, indigo coat glinting in the light. Denvy hid his alarm behind a cough, trying not to stare at the young prince's replaced leg, severed at the hip-joint. Briefly the prince glanced his way, a slight frown touching his lips before he straightened, tail twirling back and forth.

"Rythrya Blessings, Queen Nixlye."

"Prince Ryojin." Nixlye inclined her head. "How are you, my dear old friend?"

A boisterous laugh flowed from the prince, and he propped his paws on his hips. "Old friend? You're making me feel as ancient as Father! We have been well, thank you. Father has been much better since Jythal fixed his lungs." Ryojin glanced down at the Human, who rolled his eyes. "And he has finally given up smoking."

"Good to hear." Nixlye turned to Obakjen, waggling a finger. "Jythal will be pleased."

"I was fine!" Obakjen snorted. "Just a bit winded."

"Father, you almost died. I could not have looked after the shop myself." Ryojin's ears tweaked back.

Obakjen huffed, turning sharply he stomped off, slipping behind the curtain. Ryojin's air-gill's flattened around his neck. "Sorry. He is getting *old* for a Human in Utillia. I do not know how much longer his lungs will last. I keep asking him to make the trip to Pennadot."

Nixlye shook her head. "He was born here, Ryojin. You cannot ask him to go a land he knows nothing about."

"That is true, I suppose." Ryojin's mechanical leg hissed with steam as it moved, whirring and grinding with gears. "So, do you need the usual, my dear?"

Nixlye nodded. "Could you double it, though?"

"Ah. Not expecting to come back for a while?"

"Probably not."

Ryojin nodded. He shifted across to the overstuffed shelves, sorting through the contents.

Clive suddenly burst out, "Your leg is made of iron!"

Ryojin paused and looked down. He laughed softly as he placed a few items into a bag and handed them to Nixlye. "Yes, it is. Keen eye you have there, lad."

"How did it happen? Was it painful? Did a giant fish eat it?"

Ryojin's laughter sounded once more. "It was quite painful as I recall, though, alas, no giant fish ate it. That would have been quite epic. I lost it helping that queen right there," Ryojin gestured at Nixlye, "escape from the evil clutches of the Iposti."

Nixlye snorted. "I recall it the other way around. I saved your pretty little tail."

"No, no, it was all me."

Nixlye rolled her eyes and smirked up at Denvy. "It was me. I saved *him*."

Ryojin's arms spread wide. "I'm the resident mechanic of Ishabal. If a limb needs replacing, I'm the go-to-Kattamont for the job."

Nixlye graced Denvy with a wince. "Many Scavengers tend to lose limbs burning-sea diving. I worry for Aaldryn often. Ryojin is kept quite busy. He is the best in the business."

"Whooooa!" Clive climbed onto the table, picking up the nearest odd-looking device. Denvy clapped a paw over his face with a groan. He really had to start teaching Clive proper manners. "You make all this stuff! How does it work?"

Ryojin gently plucked the pair of goggles from Clive's hands and kindly set them around the boy's head. "Like most things in Utillia, machines either run off Mist or wind. Here, in the Outer Sectors, Mist is all we have. We don't rely upon the Simoon for our power; that is Iposti nonsense. We choose to power ourselves. My machines all run off Mist."

"So your leg is Mist powered," Denvy mused. His people had become ingenious in the time he had been away. He felt a small ball of pride growing in his stomach as he studied the young prince. Without the Zaprexes to guide them, the Kattamont civilization might have collapsed, but, looking around Ishabal, he saw a thriving world. It was mayhap not the cleanest, safest, or happiest of homes, but his people had built something, at least, out of the ashes of war.

Ryojin nodded. "Mist comes in three different forms. The vapour that farmers capture, the purified liquid that runs sand-ships, and its hardened state." The prince tugged out a string of white jewels from his hip-bags. "It's a trade secret, the use of Mist's jewelled form." He tapped the stones against his leg. "Have to crank up the old leg every couple hours, but it gets you around better than a piece of wood."

"I imagine your services are highly sought after."

Ryojin sighed. He rubbed a paw through his air-gills. "There's a reason we're living in the Outer Sector. The Ruling Prides are very persistent."

"Aaldryn and Jythal's invitation still stands, by the way," Nixlye said. "They would be thrilled were you to join their Brotherhood, and I honoured if you would join our Pride. And you know Mother; she would do anything to stick a thorn in the side of the Ruling Prides."

He shrugged sheepishly. "I know, and I am grateful for the offer." His gaze shifted to the curtain across the entrance into the shack. "Father cannot travel anymore with his lungs. He needs me here. He would wish me to go, but I cannot leave him."

"You are a very responsible lad." Denvy smiled warmly. Ryojin glanced his way, studying him once more. Likely the young prince was baffled at his lack of mane and the atrophy of his muscles. He was in quite a dishevelled state.

"You have the most stunning fur colour, sir."

Denvy blinked in surprise. That was not what he had expected to come out of the prince's mouth.

Clive laughed. "Everyone says that about Khwaja Denvy! It's so funny."

"Well, he does." Ryojin ruffled Clive's hair. "Are you Nixlye's new prince?"

"Sun above, no," Denvy chortled. "I am an old stray they kindly saved from poachers."

"It was amazing." Clive bounced on the table.

"How would you know?" Nixlye tweaked the boy's ear. "You were unconscious."

"Well...well..." Clive pouted. "Khwaja Denvy, can I have these glasses?" Switching tactics, Clive waved his arm about dramatically.

Denvy sighed, catching the boy before he fell off the table.

"They're actually night-vision goggles," Ryojin responded kindly. "Most Humans cannot see in the dark." He slipped the goggles off Clive's head. "So these were designed for you. They're rather handy in a tight spot, I hear. Lots of scavengers use them."

"Interesting." Denvy raised his brow. "Messengers have something similar."

Ryojin rubbed his cheek. "Well, I might have stolen the design off a Messenger passing through."

"Ah."

"We tend to do that." Ryojin looked around the market and up into the heights of the Zaprex turret. "We steal from everything. It is as if we are trying to find ourselves again. And, until we do, we will keep searching."

"Can I have them, Khwaja Denvy?" Clive pulled on his sleeve. "Please, please, please!"

He wanted to say no, really he did, but he had lost his ability to deny his children a long time ago. Perhaps that was his problem. Reaching under his poncho, Denvy fiddled for his pouch of jewels and pulled out a small ruby, handing it to Ryojin.

The prince raised an eyebrow. "Ah, this is more than enough."

Denvy shrugged. "Perhaps it will help you and your father through the winter." He hoisted Clive off the table, setting him down gently. The happy boy pulled his goggles over his head proudly and beamed. "Now I look like I really belong here!"

"Indeed, you do." Denvy chuckled. "Come along, let's find your sisters and get something to eat."

"Oh!" Ryojin cast about. "I'll come with you." He ducked his head through the curtain into the shack, giving a yell. "Father, I'm just taking my break. Watch the shop, please."

Beside the *Lawless Child,* their little dhow[7] sand-ship was barely visible. But for its shimmering rainbow sails, lit up with Mist, Jarvis was sure it would have been swallowed up by the immense ships surrounding it. He had a small bit of pride though, sitting in his stomach, as he stared at the dhow Aaldryn had managed to wrangle out of the dock manager for a fair price. It was a sweet little sand-ship, if a bit worn out. Jarvis ruffled the feathers of his scarf. He had once been a farmer boy of the Wynnila Basin, a simple Plains lad, clad in a summer frock. Now he was preparing to be a sailor of the burning-sea. He could hear his mother's voice, as though it were the soft wind brushing his hair aside, kissing his cheek, telling him that no one truly knew the steps of their own path.

Zafiashid's tail fell over his head playfully and he shivered at the warmth of her feathers. The queen swept up beside him, looming under the light of the Mist lantern she held in a paw. Jythal grabbed his arm abruptly, yanking him out of her reach and holding him protectively against his midriff.

"Mother, please stop playing with our new prince."

Zafiashid huffed. "You are no fun, Jythal."

"Play with someone who will fight back fairly." Jythal made a shooing motion with a paw.

"Fine. Fine." Zafiashid stalked away, her tail twirling as she turned to Aaldryn and Titus who were shifting Mist supplies into the little dhow's galley.

Jythal licked his paw and smoothed Jarvis' hair. Jarvis scrunched up his face. "I'm fine."

"That isn't the problem. She got her scent all over you."

"Is that a bad thing?"

Jythal shrugged. "No. It marks you as under her protection, but Nixlye would prefer it to be *her* scent. Queens tend to be territorial, especially when they live in such close proximity like Zafiashid and Nixlye."

"How do they work it out, then?"

"Nixlye is half Human. That makes a considerable difference." Jythal took his arm. "Come, I'll help you collect your things."

The Sun had sunk low in the horizon and Jythal's colouring stood out even more distinctly without his parasol to obscure him. As they

---

7 Dhow – a sand-ship with a maximum crew of twelve.

walked together, eyes followed them intently, some envious, others curious. Jarvis was almost glad the prince was blind, unable to see the stares.

Jarvis staggered, his usually loose bionic limbs seizing up suddenly as the philepcon liquid that moved them sparked in alarm. He choked out a gasp, clutching at his throat.

"Jarvis? Jarvis are you all right?"

He panted, a flush of sweat rushing over his skin as his metal hull repolarised, aligning itself once more. The whole process took barely a few seconds, but it was blindingly painful as the nano-bots refocused. He rested against Jythal, clutching the Kattamont's paw, blinking against the dazzling lights of his optical lenses.

"Whoa," he whispered. "That was weird."

"What happened?"

"Something threw my systems out of alignment."

"Are you all right now?"

Jarvis focused, centring in on himself. It was his damaged chest that registered, and the faint alarm that was still bleeping red against his lenses, though he had been ignoring it for so long it had become part of his vision. Jarvis nodded, only to slap his forehead. Jythal could not see visual cues.

"Yeah. Yeah."

Jythal gave his head a pat. "Perhaps you are still recovering."

He hoped that was the case.

They found Titus lounging on a crate of supplies, his cloak wrapped tightly around him. Even the thinnest rays of sunlight were enough to cause him discomfort. The Hunter's gaze flicked their way. He smiled in greeting and Jarvis sheepishly scrubbed the back of his neck as he hugged the pack of gear gathered from the *Lawless Child*.

"Got everything, Little Weasel?

He nodded. "I think so."

Jarvis looked up at Jythal as he shifted, and the planks beneath them groaned. His eyes were drawn to the darkness between the cracks of the harbour's interlinking rows. Every so often, the swirling breaths of the burning-sea would hiss through the gaps. It was as though the ancient sand was whispering a reminder that it was there, below them, waiting for its moment to consume them.

Jarvis shook off the eeriness and scratched his temple, wishing the red spot on his optical lens would vanish. He should have asked the Key more about being a Changeling when he had had the chance.

"You finally have your own sand-ship, brother," Jythal joked as Aaldryn joined them.

Zafiashid laughed. "That's just what I was telling him. He didn't think it was funny."

"It isn't," Aaldryn grouched. "It's a dhow."

Jarvis pushed through the Kattamonts, beaming. "I think it's magnificent."

Zafiashid wrapped an arm around her son, hugging him to her chest. He did not pull away, though it was amusing to see the taller prince bend his legs to accommodate the queen.

"A sand-ship needs a name. You must name her."

"Since Jarvis likes her so much, why don't you let him name her?" Jythal's unseeing eyes sought his position and Jarvis cocked a small smile. He liked to think that to Jythal he smelt like the sweet scent of Zaprex crystals and that was how the rune doctor always knew where to turn his head to.

"Well…" Jarvis rubbed his chin. "Something Kelib. For Ki'b."

"You are so sweet," Zafiashid purred.

"Oh!" Jarvis leapt up onto the edge of the dock's railing, gazing down at their sand-ship, swamped in size by the larger *Lawless Child.* "How about *Cor'Qwnpr?*"

"No idea what that means." Aaldryn frilled his air-gills.

"*Silver Slasher* in Common Basic." Jarvis frowned. "You know: Cor for the Cor River Network in Pennadot. Cor means silver, and Qwnpr is usually the word used for a slashing object in Kelib, like a blade, or a dagger, or even a farmer's sickle. Changes meaning depending on how you pronounce it, according to Ki'b—"

Jarvis glanced from one to the other. "Wait. You don't know any Kelib? Not even a little bit?" Jarvis crossed his arms stoutly. His father had insisted he learn some of the tongue of the Kelibs, at least to help in appeasing the few trees on their farm. Contented trees, his father said, meant a contented farm. They always had an ample supply of lumber whenever they asked, because they respected their trees.

Jarvis frowned, glancing at Titus. His master's black eyes shared his gaze. Titus shook his head and Jarvis breathed easier. Titus knew how much wished he could return home, as though nothing had transpired to lead him here. The Hunter had family too, and he was just as far from his home.

Zafiashid startled him with a laugh. "Lad, I don't think even the Kelibs in Utillia remember how to speak Kelib. They have been here for generations. Whatever roots they had connecting them to Pennadot have long gone."

"Still." Aaldryn clapped his paws. "I like it. Strong name, Jarvis. She'll sail us well with a strong name. You've got to treat your sand-ships like family. That's the key to living on the burning-sea."

He could do that. The family Khwaja Denvy had given him might not have been the one he had been born into, but it was just as precious now. He could make a sand-ship part of that family. Jarvis gripped the pummel of his elemental-blade, heading for the stairs that led to the jetty. "You need to teach me how to use it, Aaldryn."

"That's Captain Aaldryn to you." The prince clapped his shoulder. His hull should have absorbed the force of the Kattamont's strength; the protector bot within him was capable of dissipating immense amounts of force, even without his gravity bubble activated. So the surprise of finding himself on his knees, sprawled out, alarmed not just him, but those around him too.

"Jarvis!"

His hands went to his head as the red he had been ignoring burst in a shattering eruption against his skull, scratching down his spine like needles. He was momentarily aware of an intrusion into his mind, not unlike the Dragon invading his firewalls, but it was released through in a torrent as its code was recognized. His gaze snapped to the Zaprex turret in alarm. Information, jumbled together in panic, flooded into him. Titus' arms, strong and steady, held him up by his shoulders, and he sensed Zafiashid crouching, her heavy paw on his arm.

"Is it your wound?" she asked softly.

He shook his head. It was worse. So much worse than any old wound. Tears trickled down his cheeks. Death. A friend was dying—a friend he did not even know. The turret.

"The gravity is destabilizing. The turret is failing." He covered his face. "I'm sad."

DENVY MAZ - DREAM MASTER OF THE NORTHLANDS

CHAPTER ELEVEN

I hope my gift soothes your anger.
Goodness knows how you can stand drinking the stuff.
It's horrendous.

Today was a momentous day.
Please do raise a toast, my dear, to our future.
I truly do not know if the energy produced by the rotation of the
Northlands will be enough to create the same symphony as the
Towers, but the gravity should hold long enough to keep the other
lands in orbit stable.

By my predictions the Secondary Realm will begin collapsing some
centuries from now. They'll see the signs—I hope. If we're not here,
to warn them.
It gives us some stability for now.
Well…
As much stability as you can have in war.
I am sorry, my love, that no one ever listened to your warnings—
about the core, about the danger lurking within.
We just saw a broken world in need of fixing.
You saw the mouse trap.

Private Communications Link.
Utillian Time 5:24AM.
Signal: Strong.
Upload: Completed.
Do you wish to send?
Send Beer. Yes.
I would just love to defrag eight cartons of beer
to my bonding partner thank you…

Denvy was surprised by Ryojin's strength as the indigo Kattamont grabbed his arm to help him navigate the press of bodies blocking their path. Nixlye had already wheeled ahead some distance, her solid metal chair and sharp tongue aiding her greatly in pushing her way through the crowds. Sol-cycles surrounded by Humans and Kelibs had made Denvy forget how strong his own race was. Teaching himself to be gentle, slow, and kindly had taken a considerable effort, and now it was all unravelling around him.

They found Ki'b and Penny, both bubbling with excitement. Ki'b showed off a pouch of new stones, counting each rock until Penny snapped at her and Denvy was forced to break them apart. Ki'b had chosen well, though. Her stones carried the scents of Pennadot, of the deep earth below the forests, and the high peaks of the Ovin-tu Mountains. It seemed the trade for Pennadotian earth was a commodity even in Utillia. Humans managed to make anything worth selling into trade.

Denvy squinted up at the sky-sea. The Sun was already sinking low, barely holding itself in the sky-sea long enough for there to be light to live by, and already the city was beginning to glow with Mist-powered lamps, hissing with steam from the pipes connecting them to the major stations below the boardwalks. As they strolled along, Ryojin jubilantly explained the workings of the gigantic cranes, and the elevators up to the levels above their reach. It seemed Nixlye's assessment of Ryojin was correct. He was a mechanic of high calibre, having worked on much of the city's maintenance.

"I hear the Wind Cities are even more magnificent." Ryojin looked up at a Mist lantern. "But the Iposti control the Simoon, so it does not surprise me. There is only so much we know how to do with Mist."

"What you have achieved already is admirable," Denvy said. "You should be immensely proud. The Zaprexes would be honoured by the legacy you are providing."

"Really?" It was Nixlye who answered, a frown deepening the creases of her forehead. "You think so? You don't think they'd be upset that we're cutting up their cities to create our own?"

Denvy shook his head. "Great civilizations are often built on the backs of others. If there is one thing the Zaprexes desired most it was to provide those they loved with the building blocks to survive. And I think you are all doing that splendidly."

Nixlye sagged back into her wheelchair, breathing out. Denvy gave her shoulder a gentle pat. Knowing the young queen now, it was likely she had worried often that they were trespassing upon holy ground, especially during the long days when Aaldryn was diving the deep veins of the burning-sea.

"It is getting late." Ryojin ruffled his air-gills, as if trying to settled them down against the compliment. "I should get back to Father. He gets so befuddled without me these days." He reached out a paw, brushing Nixlye's cheek lightly. "Stay safe, my queen. Perhaps when you return I will join your princes' Brotherhood."

"I would like that, Ryo. Continuing our adventures together would be lovely."

The prince nodded. He turned to Denvy and smiled. Denvy held out his arm and the prince seized it, returning his fierce grip in a brief test of strength.

"It was an honour to meet you, sir."

Ryojin tangled Clive's hair playfully, eliciting a giggle, before he jogged away down a bouncing bridge. Nixlye's chair wheeled up beside

Denvy, creaking against the boardwalk planks. He looked down at her.

She bit her lip, holding in laughter. "I think we should keep that yoke on you. I fear for all the princes and neutrals in Utillia if we took it off. You might con them all into thinking you're a gentleman."

"But I am a gentleman." Baffled at her assessment, Denvy scratched his chin, pondering what he could have done to make her think otherwise.

Nixlye's hands slapped onto the arms of her chair abruptly. They tightened as the planks beneath them shifted to one side, her chair tilting as the wheels wobbled. The Mist-powered lantern above them burst in a crackle, raining down hissing liquid. Denvy snatched up Penny and Clive, running swiftly across the nearest bridge as the surface below them cracked and shattered. He heard Ki'b's cry, faint against the echoing burst of wood and metal about them as everything dropped. Clive and Penny's screams were muffled against his chest as they all plunged into the shifting sands of the burning-sea. The heat took a sudden, choking hold of his throat as he struggled against the current. As his head broke the surface he caught a brief glance of the buckling underside of the city, quaking under an invisible force as the burning-sea shuddered. Debris fell around them. Denvy threw Clive over a plank. Penny clambered for it, too, gripping its sides. He lost himself under the sand. Darkness fell around him, richer than he had known even within the box of the Twizels, thicker than any night without moons. The roaring of the sand swallowed him.

Paws clamped around his arms, bladed nails digging deeply into his skin, ripping through the flesh. He pushed against the sand—an effortless attempt, but he could try, shaking his fur as his head came loose and the light of a Mist lantern blinded him momentarily.

"I have no idea what Mother means," Nixlye's voice called. "You're heavier than a mountain!"

"Don't let him go! I've got the cubs." Ryojin skidded into the light, his iron leg hissing steam as he knelt, releasing Clive and Penny.

Denvy blinked away sand, staring at Nixlye lying flat over the boards, her arms trembling as she held him above the surface. "Your legs," he choked out.

"Ki'b's got them. I've got you."

Ryojin joined Nixlye, throwing in his weight and Denvy winced as the prince's claws drew blood. He wrapped his own paws around the prince's arms and breathed out as the sand around him loosened and he was hauled up onto the boards of the bobbing jetty, below the top levels of Ishabal. He sagged heavily. Nixlye dragged herself to her discarded wheelchair, climbing onto it. Her wide eyes stared above them. Distant screams echoed beyond them, in the burning-sea itself and above the city.

"Oh, by the Currents." Nixlye swept her arms around his cubs, dragging them against her wheel-chair. "Null-zone! The sector is collapsing."

The erasing wave grew. The ancient beams beneath the small city, holding the boardwalks aloft, swayed and bent like dancing branches, beginning to splinter with the movement. The Zaprex turret itself, looming over them, released an intense groan, its arches of shimmering glass leaning as their foundations dissolved. The children screamed, covering their ears in horror. Denvy grabbed for Nixlye's chair, scooping her clean from its confines. She yelped.

"No! Wait!"

"No time!" He bounded over the fallen debris, turning back to grab Penny's hand.

Ryojin heaved Ki'b over a collapsing beam. "Run! Get back to the *Lawless*. Go! Run!"

Denvy glanced behind them. He could ignore the shaking planks, the shattering houses collapsing on either side, the swinging beams he had to duck under and swerve past, but not the rippling of the Zaprex turret's surface as it teetered. It was going to burst. Dear Sun on High—it was going to shatter into a thousand shards before the null-zone could swallow it whole and they would never outrun it.

"Null-zone," Aaldryn spluttered out. "Here? Now? That's impossible!"

Jarvis felt Zafiashid shift from his side. He wished she had not, the blazing pain in his skull intruded again, sending flashes across his vision. Focusing on the information blaring across his optical lenses taxed his tensed muscles.

"Get to the *Lawless*, now!" Zafiashid barked.

"No!" Aaldryn caught her arm. "Nixlye is still out there, with Denvy and his cubs."

The queen froze, her chest rising in rapid breaths as her air-gills spread. A conflicted, pained look crossed her face. Jarvis struggled to his feet. "We'll go. We'll get them. You get back to the *Lawless*. Get out of here—"

He staggered back against Master Titus as the surface shifted beneath them. Far into the city, like a geyser that had been released, sand tore through the houses, shooting debris into the air. Another bellowed down the docks, cracking through an arc of the Zaprex turret. The glistening shards of the ancient machine caught the last rays of the Sun, at once momentarily beautiful and ultimately dreadful as the immense pieces of glass and iron crashed down upon the sand-ships and houses, and the patrons of the markets.

Zafiashid grabbed Jythal by the wrist, dragging him across cracking planks as the harbour buckled. Jarvis focused on the wave coming towards them, splintering wood and metal, throwing bodies into the air, and shattering the crates and cranes down on the dock as it approached. Screams filled the air. He was snatched up by Titus, but his eyes refused to leave the sight as they caught every terrifying detail. Down the stairs they raced to their dhow. The boat was being tossed about on the rough sand-waves, straining on its anchor chain.

"Get in!" Aaldryn swung himself onto the deck and bounded towards the array of controls. "Hoist the anchor, Titus. Jarvis, get those ropes! Hurry!"

He scrambled to obey, loosening the ropes binding the *Silver Slasher* to the jetty. A bellowing groan erupted around them and he covered his ears, cursing at his newly-sensitive hearing. He watched as nearby trading vessels caught the swell of an immense sand-wave. Jarvis went slack, his mind blanking out in awe as a huge metal sand-ship bent to the will of the burning-sea. Iron cables snapped and thousands of crates stacked on its deck spilt loose. His protector bot panicked and he swept out his sword, slashing the lines of their dhow.

"Aaldryn! Go! Go!"

The prince swept the controls into action and Jarvis caught himself in his gravity bubble as the sand-ship beneath him ripped forward in a burst of Mist. The ignited burn blinded him momentarily. When the flash faded, he wished he was still unable to see. The giant crates rained down around them from the slowly falling trading vessel. He clung to the edge of the dhow as it was jostled. Aaldryn swerved around the crates, which burst open as they impacted the burning-sea, tossing Pennadotian produce into the sand. He peeled himself from the railing, clambering towards the control deck. They flew beneath the boardwalks, veering around the arching foundation beams of the city.

"Where would they be?" Aaldryn bellowed.

"The markets! The girls wanted to buy some stones," Jarvis yelled back. He forcefully filtered out from his vision the sight of those drowning in the burning-sea around them, scanning only for figures he knew. A thick darkness was closing in, like that which had consumed *Bez-at:_Who_Lingers_by_Water* —a darkness of deletion.

"What's happening to everything?"

"Null-zone." Aaldryn spun the wheel. "Swallows everything whole. We've got to get out before the whole sector collapses in on itself or we'll be caught up in the disintegration process."

Jarvis shivered. They should not have been here, ploughing into the death of a turret. The data of the desktop grid was dissolving around Ishabal and the process was creating such an enormous energy build up it was destroying even things not part of the desktop itself.

He stared down in alarm at his skin, watching as flakes of the brown membrane brushed off into the air. Aaldryn was right. They would be caught up in the disintegration. What if they were too late? What if Ki'b was already gone?

"Master Titus!" Jarvis turned sharply. "We have to—"

The breath left his lungs as a monstrous, swelling shape blocked the last of the Sun's rays, leaping forth from the roof of a house towards them. The Ki'rayh! What was it doing here, now, in this place? Why was it taking the risk to come here?

Jarvis clutched at the small prism under his cloak. Alarms flared through his skull. Was it after the Map piece the Key had instructed him to take to the House of Flames?

The Ki'rayh swirled elegantly through the beams, its mantle of shadows flickering and smoking like black flames. With a screech it landed against the tail-end of the *Silver Slasher* in the shape of a bird, talons and beak gleaming golden like some prideful trophy of its high rank.

Titus quivered. His hands wrapped around the hilt of his blade and his eyes narrowed into thin slits. "Figured it'd come out now."

"Master Titus!" Jarvis ran across the small deck, following the Hunter who lunged, swinging his ovi-sword. The force from its immense size created a great draught of wind, tipping the dhow. Aaldryn yelled in frustration as they scraped past a fallen beam.

"Stop! For Rythrya's sake, take your stone-giant sword someplace it doesn't make whirl-winds around my Titan! I'm trying to save my mate! Wait—is that Torka?"

"Torka, hmmm?" Titus leered. "Hey, Twizel. Sounds like you've got a pet name. I call you out! Come here and kiss my sword!"

Jarvis winced, throwing up a shield of reflective colour as a flurry of bladed bones scratched their way across the deck. He stared at one that hissed with acid. The Ki'rayh screeched, diving at Titus. His master took the brunt of the force with the edge of his stone-giant blade, the grin over his slowly dissolving features manic, crazed, and—dare he say it?—happy.

The Hunter swung up a boot, smashing it through the clattering bones and hanging flesh that held the pieces of the Twizel together, causing innards to spill across the deck. Jarvis scrambled back as the Ki'rayh flew past. His proximity alarm blared. It might have snatched him in its beak or talons, ripping him from the deck despite his gravity bubble rooting him down, had Titus' blade not landed firmly beside him like a shield. The stone-giant blade missed him by a hair's breadth, but he had never felt more relieved to see the immense weapon. He knew the stories. Messengers did not take on Twizels alone without their squads to back them up. Only Hunters did. Only his master would. This was what Titus did; this was why his master lived.

The Twizel made another pass, taunting them. Then it billowed out over the sand towards the city. Titus dodged past, snatching up his sword. "I'll draw it away."

"But, Master, this sector is collapsing—"

"Don' yeh worry about me, Little Weasel. Find the old man." Titus bounced over the edge of the dhow.

Jarvis spluttered out a string of curses. He scrambled up, watching as the Hunter vanished into the city in pursuit. Slamming a fist against the railing, he yelled out, "It wants you to chase it! It's playing with us! Can't you see that, you idiot!"

The sand-ship lurched suddenly. Jarvis yelped as the *Silver Slasher* barely missed a section of falling city. The force of the sand-wave sent him tumbling overboard before his protector bot could arrest the motion. His reaction time was still Human, but he landed firmly on his feet, swinging back and forth on a metal beam that bobbed on the surface of the burning-sea. Jarvis curled against the crashing noise as thick planks fell around him. Wind ripped through the debris, scattering it. The coils of an elemental force wrapped around him. It was warm against his hull, pulling him back from danger and sharply onto the deck of the *Silver Slasher*. He heard Khamsin whisper, so brief against his ears.

Do try not to fall overboard, Changeling.

But he had seen, through the darkness, a flash of light he was familiar with, for it had been one of the first things he had set eyes on when released from the confines of the box. It had filled him with the greatest relief then, and even more so now. The belief in a realm not of his own—Khwaja Denvy.

"Aaldryn! Over there! It's Khwaja Denvy's water-sword." He pointed. "Hurry! Please!"

Aaldryn swung the wheel, releasing another stream of Mist though the sail and it lit the area in a glistening of rainbows. Jarvis bit back his horror at the sight of bodies strewn throughout the burning-sea. Aaldryn ploughed through them. "Get the lines ready."

He rushed to do so, cursing each time his feet bounced on the deck and his gravity bubble dislodged him. All the practice he had done, his training, felt void in the panic of the moment as he struggled against the ropes. Aaldryn clambered down from the controls to join him.

"Wait—who is keeping the dhow stable?"

"Khamsin," Aaldryn shouted.

The Kattamont snatched rune stones from his hip-bags and cast them through the air. Jarvis winced as they burst into hot, blue flames, swirling around each other like dazzling wisps in the deep darkness surrounding them. Relief filled his lungs in a rush as he heard Ki'b's voice screaming his name. He turned towards the sound. She was there. His lenses focused on her where she balanced on a wobbling piece of debris, clutching on to a Kattamont he did not know.

"Ryojin!" Aaldryn grabbed a line, twirling it above his head. "Thank the Rythrya. Hurry. Catch this!"

The Kattamont grasped the line, dragging the piece of debris closer. Jarvis caught sight of Clive and Penny gripping tightly onto the plank of wood. He called out to them and Clive looked up, beaming brightly.

"Jarvis. You came for us."

"Always, little brother." He reached out and over the railing. Clive used him roughly as a ladder, calling for Penny to climb up and she did quickly. She was sobbing as she landed on the deck. Clive swung himself up, running to her side, trying to calm her. Jarvis hurried over as Aaldryn set Ki'b down on the deck. She wrapped her arms around his waist.

"I was scared."

"You're safe now." He tried to sound reassuring.

Ryojin, an indigo-pelted prince, with a tail frilled out in stunning greens, stayed bobbing on the debris and, curious, Jarvis watched for the reason. Aaldryn leapt over the edge of the dhow, landing beside the Kattamont.

"Nixlye! Where is Nixlye?"

"She was with Denvy. I lost sight of them trying to keep the cubs together."

"Jarvis, can you see Nixlye and Denvy?" Aaldryn cried out.

Jarvis scanned the area, narrowing his eyes against the rune stone lights. Debris cracked off from above them, raining down into the burning-sea. The longer they lingered, the more danger they were in. He froze, spotting something, and he pointed. "Right there, Aaldryn! Coming towards us. She's right there."

Aaldryn ran across the surface of the burning-sea and dragged at a thick wedge of metal, pulling Nixlye to him. She grabbed his paws, shaking sand from her air-gills.

"Denvy! Denvy went under. I couldn't stop him," she cried. "He was so heavy. And he was so tired. He was keeping me up."

Jarvis' eyes widened and he turned, pin-pointing the area she had just vacated. He ran, tying a line around his waist. The hesitation was momentary, barely stalling him as he plunged over the edge of the dhow and into the shifting sands of the burning-sea. The impact was dazzling, like thousands of tiny needles intruding against his metal hull as it absorbed the force. He struggled against the crushing weight of the sand, moving his philepcon liquid through his muscles, charging each push. His eyes caught every movement within the sand, folding back the darkness like it was a curtain. A paw waved in front of him and he fumbled for it. Everything was slow, the sand so thick. He screamed silently in frustration as he tried again. This time his hands latched around Khwaja Denvy's wrists. He heaved backwards, feeling his body strain as the protector bot whirred in a burst of energy.

The old Kattamont had kept him alive in the darkness, in the terrible box. His voice, deep and gravelled, had been the only thing in the heartless world he had been shoved into that had told him to live.

You have to keep living, Khwaja Denvy. You have to see Zinkx again.

The spark activated down his backbone, the protector bot within him spreading out and down his limbs. It felt as though one of his father's heavy winter coats had fallen over him, and was now moulding itself over his skin as his warm metal hull expanded, forming a full exoskeleton.

The burst of energy pulsed around him, swelling the sand back, just enough, he realized, to pull them both out. Paws grabbed them. Aaldryn and Ryojin dragged them towards the *Silver Slasher* and onto the deck. Ki'b flung herself onto him but he barely felt her heavy weight. His body was buzzing. The world looked eerily clearer. His heard turned sharply toward Aaldryn and he blinked. Had he not been pinned down by Ki'b, he would have scrambled away in alarm at the sight of the halo of wind that rose from the Kattamont prince. It shifted, coiling like a snake, a triangular head forming. Yellow eyes peered down at him, unblinking and curious.

It is all right, Changeling. What you are seeing is the Secondary Realm and how it interacts with the Primary Realm. You are currently in your protector bot mode; you need to deactivate it.

Khamsin's voice. He was seeing Khamsin's apparition surrounding Aaldryn. Jarvis wiped his face, only to feel a veil-like shield coating his features.

"You've got to see yourself, brother," Aaldryn chuckled. "You look like a legendary machine from Nixlye's tales."

"We've got to go." Jarvis scrambled to his feet. "Aaldryn, we have to go now!"

He pointed through the darkness beyond them. The null-zone was coming. Could the others not see it? The data eroding before their eyes? The desktop grid was vanishing and he had never seen anything more terrifying; not even a Twizel was this frightening. This was the terror their world faced if the Key did not get its Map piece, if the Borders stopped spinning—a death of total blackness, of deletion, of nothing.

"Aaldryn!" Jarvis tripped over Khwaja Denvy. "Get us out of here."

The Kattamont scrambled for the controls, but already Khamsin had sent the vessel speeding forward in a burst of wind, ignoring the direction of the sails. Jarvis winced as the mast groaned with the strain. He was caught in a weak grasp and he looked back, finding Khwaja Denvy's gaze.

"Thank you, Jarvis, for coming back for me."

That was unexpected. It was if the old man had not believed anyone would bother. Jarvis frowned. "Sir, you are the reason we survived that box. I will always, always come back for you."

He might have become a Messenger but it did not mean he had to accept their belief of leaving soldiers behind to die, to never turn back on the field of battle for fear of falling prey to Twizels. He was still Jarvis of the Plains People, a farmer's son. He would always come back.

The small city was hanging together by threads of metal.

He heard Clive's shout. "Why does it look like it's raining?"

It did. His little sibling was right. It looked as though it was raining, only the rain was moving upwards, and it was not rain—they were tiny particles of data being lost as the null-zone approached. He was glad he was not the one who would have to explain to Clive that they were breathing the remains of people. Jarvis clutched at the railing as they launched through the air and landed roughly against a dune. He cursed under his breath as Aaldryn swung them around a dislodged house sticking out of the burning-sea. Their path changed abruptly, towards the harbour, or what was left of it, and suddenly the sea of debris became overshadowed by the immense, looming fixtures of the trading vessels. Did Aaldryn see them? They were heading right for them.

"The trading vessels!" Jarvis screeched. "They're blocking our path!" The huge sand-ships had formed a wall, crushed and bent against each other. There had been no hope of them leaving the harbour after the waves had dislodged them. They were approaching too fast. The dhow would be crushed upon impact.

"I can see that." Aaldryn heaved down on the sails, strapping them down. "Ryo! Keep everyone tied to the deck."

"What are you doing?' Jarvis scrambled after him as he switched levers and began to crack around on another smaller wheel. It wheezed and whirred with each spin.

"Hold on!" Aaldryn howled. Jarvis slammed back onto his rump as wings spread out from the sides of the dhow, launching them into the air. Mist ignited down the sails on either sides of the sand-ship, boosting their flight and Jarvis covered his face as wind erupted from Aaldryn. The underbelly of the *Silver Slasher* scraped against a trading vessel, the loud screech drowning out all thought but that of survival. Jarvis held his breath. They landed with a thud on the other side, swelling up sand. Aaldryn collapsed back. Nixlye called out in alarm, trying to move towards him. Instead the indigo Kattamont quickly scrambled up.

"Aaldryn?"

"Ryo, can you get the controls? I can't get us to the *Lawless*. I have to stop." He curled up, clutching his head. Ryojin briefly touched his shoulder before grabbing the helm, swinging the dhow in the direction of a gathering of vessels far out into the dunes. It was so sudden Jarvis barely caught the gleam of the iron cable in the darkness. His reflexes moved him forward, running for the Kattamont prince at the controls, but he was too far away. Before his eyes the feline was ripped from the deck and dragged overboard as dozens of metal cables surrounded their sand-ship. His hand was still outstretched in startled alarm when Ki'b's cries reached him and he spun, seeing swarms of wreckage swirling towards them, dragged by a sand-dune wave.

"Aaldryn. We're not free of the gravity," he shouted. "Do something!"

"Get us loose." Aaldryn shoved him.

Jarvis dashed down onto the lower deck, ripping out his colour sword. He headed for the nearest cable, swinging his blade.

Nixlye's hand grabbed his ankle. "Where is Ryojin?"

"I wasn't fast enough." He shook his head. "I'm sorry."

Nixlye scrambled forward. "No. Ryojin. No! No. Please!" she screamed over the edge of the railing. Denvy's arms wrapped around her waist, pulling her back against him. The two landed roughly against the deck as the sand-ship heaved to one side. Jarvis hacked at the iron cable dragging them back into the null-zone's grasp. He spared an anxious glance at the wall of vessels they were being hauled toward. Ki'b joined him, bloodying her fingers as she tore through the metal with her bare hands. The crack echoed around them. Jarvis threw himself over Ki'b as the cable whiplashed apart, breaking against the rails of the dhow. The *Silver Slasher* burst forth in a rush of wind. He dared to peer over Ki'b's head, up at Aaldryn. The prince looked frail against the controls, wind coiling about him as he dragged their tiny sand-ship free of the debris zone.

Nixlye clung to Denvy, sobbing into his chest. She had bloodied her claws, ripping into his fur. How he wished he could control the dhow, to let Aaldryn go to his mate in her distress. He dragged himself back onto the top deck.

"I think we're free."

Aaldryn's paws twisted around the wheel. "The *Lawless* made it out, too."

Through the burning-sea dunes, the *Lawless Child* was lit up brightly in a show of Mist, amongst the other sand-ships that had survived the ruin. Smaller dhows and life-boats bobbed against the tossing sand waves. Panicked voices and the sound of grieving met them as they moved through the gathering that had formed.

So few had made it out. Jarvis rubbed his sweating hands together.

Nixlye's weeping made it all worse. It made it even more real. His sister had cried like that when the Twizels had killed her husband. He could still remember it. Jarvis shook his head, trying to clear the memory.

The *Lawless Child's* deck was covered in crew, and they were eerily silent, faces turned to the ruins of Ishabal. Upon sighting them, they were hailed with shouts of greeting and ropes were thrown overboard—along with Master Titus, who leapt and landed on the deck of the dhow. He skidded up beside Khwaja Denvy.

"The Ki'rayh is swift on our tail. We can draw it away if we leave now."

"You're not serious," Jarvis spluttered out. They had barely made it out. He did not want to go. They were not ready—he was not ready. Leaving Ki'b, Clive, and Penny…Nixlye and Jythal?

"I am. We have to leave now."

Denvy's brow furrowed. "Titus—"

"Denvy, yeh've got stuff to do here in Utillia. Yeh do not want a Ki'rayh on yer heels. Jarvis and I can deal with it, get it back to Coltarian where it belongs. Yeh know Messenger code. We run."

Something in those words made the old man turn. Something made his shoulders sag in defeat and Jarvis wished he could reach out and reassure him that they were not running away from him. He could not, though. There was no time. Jarvis clutched at Ki'b's hand. Her eyes widened in understanding and she flung her arms around his neck, sobbing. He could barely come out with something worth saying, something that would sum up what he wished her to know. Khwaja Denvy was already clambering up the ropes to the *Lawless Child*, helping Nixlye. He was never going to get to say goodbye to him. He kissed Ki'b's forehead.

"I promise I'll come back," he whispered. "I'll come back and we'll get married."

Ki'b pressed a small, smooth rock into his hand. "Don't break your promise."

She grabbed hold of a rope and climbed hand over hand up the side of the sand-ship. Clive dodged past him, looking back with a sad, lingering glance.

"Clive. Don't do anything I wouldn't do," he yelled out. "And keep Penny close."

Aaldryn lingered at the edge for a moment, looking up at the *Lawless Child*.

"Jythal, keep them safe, brother," he shouted up, into the dim light of the lanterns.

"Stay alive," the soft reply returned.

Aaldryn turned sharply, his walk tight as he took the controls. The *Silver Slasher* swung away from the *Lawless Child*. Jarvis should not have looked back. The moment he did, he regretted the decision for he could not tear his eyes from the sight of the sand-ship bobbing on the edge of a dune, backdropped by the ruins of Ishabal dimly glowing in the distance. An uncomfortable, twisting sensation grew in his stomach as the vessel vanished on the horizon. Why did he feel that this was the last time he would ever see any of his family again? Surely it was just the natural fear of being separated from them. He closed his eyes. It had to be an illusion of the wind against his cheeks, but he could almost taste Ki'b's tears. She would have been crying by now. Perhaps they were his own tears he was tasting.

"I'll come back, Little Mountain Flower. I'll come back."

Jarvis wrapped his fingers around the last Map piece.

"I hope, Key," he whispered, "that you're worth it."

CHAPTER TWELVE

49 20 68 61 76 65 20 74 68 65 20 4b 65 79
2e 20 53 61 66 65 2e 20 4b 65 6d 65 74 2f
43 61 6c 27 70 61 73 68 27 63 6f 6f 2e 20 46
69 6e 64 69 6e 67 20 4f 73 69 72 69 73 2e
20 4c 61 73 74 20 54 72 61 6e 73 6d 69 73
73 69 6f 6e 2e 20 48 61 7a 61 6e 69 6e 2e

Exhaustion. He had not known the likes of it since he was a cub. It was debilitating and frustrating. It plagued him, even in his sleep. The lingering part of him that was vaguely awake knew he was in Zafiashid's cabin, sprawled out on her bed. His weakened chest rumbled with the infection of the persistent Human illness. It was miserable, Denvy concluded, the state he was in—simply miserable.

"You really should do something about that," an affluent voice said from behind him.

Denvy turned sharply, swaying as he stepped onto the surface of a dune. The abrupt change in scenery was disorientating. He had not experienced a dreamscape for sol-cycles. The notion that he had returned to the zone within the Secondary Realm was both elating and terrifying. The wide expanses of the burning-sea blanketed the horizon as far as he could see, and a Sunrise capped the dunes in a crystal shine, igniting tall spires in the distance. Alone beside him stood a tiny, delicate Zaprex, wings of energy fluttering rapidly enough to make the sand dance around its ankles.

"Sekhmet." His voice hitched with emotion. "Gibo!"

If Hazanin-*sama* had been the Zaprexes' embodiment of time, Sekhmet had been their finest protector, a warrior of the highest calibre, despite appearing to be anything but. The ancient being had been left in a Tower—forever protecting a world that did not want protection. The sorrow Denvy had always perceived in the sapphire eyes of the delicate cyborg was evident as it stared into his inner being, assessing him as though looking for damage done over the centuries of his life. He felt immeasurably old, weighed down by the sol-cycles that separated them. Sekhmet wore the very last thing he could recall it wearing. A simple body-suit, primed for battle, protecting a fragile body that had been grievously abused.

Antennae tweaked rearward in curiosity, and a smile graced the forlorn Zaprex's lips. Sekhmet turned towards the rising Sun. "Maahes, look at my beautiful desert. I saved Utillia, as best I could. It is up to you to finish what I started." Sekhmet drifted away, fading into the light.

Denvy held out a paw. "Gibo, please. Wait. Please stay."

"I cannot stay when I was never here, Maahes."

His hearts raced, thudding against his ribs. "Don't leave me alone. I never wanted to dream alone."

"Denvy, is that you?" The intrusion of another voice was startling. He almost jumped in alarm. It had been so long since he had linked with anyone in a dreamscape. Not since the Dreamers Who Dreamt at the House of Flames, and Titus' young wife, Rein, had he experienced the sensation of another mind linked with his own.

Nixlye stared at him in confusion, the fur of her cheeks still damp, as though she had been weeping. Tears, he was sure, shed for Ryojin— and the lives lost in Ishabal. Denvy raised his brow at the sight of her wheelchair in this dreamscape desert. Despite the situation, he smiled. The young queen was a wonder. For her to picture herself in her chair, even in her dreams, revealed how holistically accepting she was of herself. Her avatar within the Secondary Realm reflected stability. No matter how often he had worked with dreamathic Messengers who had lost limbs to the viciousness of the Trenches, always they had tried to dream themselves whole again. It was more an indictment of a society that could not accept their wounded back into its fold, than a reflection on the children he had nursed. It was refreshing to be confronted with Nixlye's unwavering steadfastness.

Denvy slowly made his way towards her, and Jythal standing silently beside her. It was peculiar indeed. He had never expected to find himself encountering the wandering minds of the two dreamathics, especially with the yoke still tight around his neck. Did the gem nexus of the two youngsters work even better in close proximity than he had thought? Perhaps it was the null-zone's displacement of the Primary Realm that had created enough residual energy for him to absorb to evade the yoke's binding properties.

"Where are we?" Jythal turned, tossing up sand around his ankles. "However did we get here?"

"Can you see, Jythal?" Denvy asked, finding himself suddenly curious.

"No. I do know we're outside, though. I can feel sand beneath my foot-paws. We're standing on the burning-sea. Wait. That should be impossible. We should be sinking!" He skipped back a few paces, air-gills hackling.

Denvy chuckled. "Anything is possible in a dreamscape."

"What is a dreamscape?" Nixlye reached out a hand, waving it around, only to pull it back in disappointment when she encountered nothing but air.

"It is the Secondary Realm's manifestation within a dreamathic's mind." Denvy rubbed the back of his neck. "I do apologise. I am not sure how, but you appear to have entered a dream I am having. Perhaps, due to the damage the yoke has done, I am unable to limit my range. As a Dream Master, my dreamathic strength requires a considerable amount of regulation."

Nixlye turned to him, shaking her head. "Actually, this is the Misfit Dream. All misfits have this dream."

"A mass dreaming?" Denvy mused aloud. That was quite fascinating. "There are very few things that can cause a mass dreaming on a large scale."

Nixlye shrugged. "I have never before been inside of the dream like this. Usually it is replayed like a hazy memory. This is remarkably realistic."

"Indeed," Jythal agreed. "Usually I see the Misfit dream as though my sight were returned to me. I know it isn't real."

"It is a true dreamscape then. It is quite often how dreamathics communicate over long distances on their own nexus." He turned toward the spires in the distance. How he wished he could reach out across the unseen web of the Data-Ways he had once wandered as a cub, so freely, like they had simply been streets to travel and not gateways across vast distances, over worlds and galaxies. Rein was out there, somewhere, listening for him, and he could not contact her to tell her that Titus was coming home.

"You say all misfits have this dream?"

Nixlye nodded. She composed herself, wiping her damp cheeks. "I have it quite often, though I have never understood its meaning."

"It has become a sort of rite of passage for misfits. Many on the *Lawless Child* have dreamt it," Jythal added. "It should come as no surprise that you, sir, would eventually dream it also."

"Interesting." Denvy hummed. Was something out there, across the burning-sea, calling to the misfit-born of Utillia, trying to draw them in? His air-gills spread slightly as a flare of sunlight caught the tips of the spires in the distance and he blinked at the sharp intensity of the dawn.

Nixlye wheeled towards him, her tail vibrating in excitement. "Where is she?"

"Who?"

"The Zaprex?" Nixlye looked around. "There is always a Zaprex in this dream. She is usually here, at the beginning, looking out across the desert. She cries. It's how misfits know that Zaprexes are not malevolent. We can feel her agony for what was lost."

A low rumbling chuckle escaped from Denvy. Of course it would stand to reason that a Kattamont would look upon a Zaprex and presume it was female. He breathed in deeply, bowing his head.

"Sekhmet is gone." Gone—not just from this dream but from the world itself.

Nixlye clapped her hands on the sides of her wheelchair and sagged back. "Bother. It would have been amazing to see her like this. You said her name is Sekhmet?"

His shoulders were heavy, but he pulled them back, ignoring the weight of the memories the name evoked. "Sekhmet was one of the Twelve Original Zaprexes—part of the Pantheon. The bonding partner of Nefertem." He could tell she wanted to know more. The thirsty little scholar inside her could have listened to him tell tales for hours, he was sure. But he had nothing to tell—not yet. She seemed to sense his hesitation, or perhaps she caught the irate flick of his tail. Either way, she did not press him.

Jythal moved up beside him. "As a Dream Master, is it possible for you to dream something into existence, beyond this realm?"

Denvy tugged on the yoke fastened around his neck. "Yes. It is likely one of the reasons my captors needed to bind me. I am quite skilled at manipulating the energy, or, as the Zaprexes would call it, the songs, of the Secondary Realm."

"Can you do it while awake?" Jythal queried.

Denvy glanced back at the white lion. "Hmm, now isn't that an interesting question. Do you daydream, young prince?"

Jythal frowned. "Yes, I suppose."

"Then I suppose I can."

"You're telling me that you could create something in a dreamscape out of energy from the Secondary Realm and bring it into existence in the Primary Realm?"

"It was one of my design features. Never seemed much of a big deal when I was cub." He settled his paws upon Nixlye's chair and crouched. "So, my dear, what is it that you see in this dream?"

She poked his nose fondly. "I see you, our seeing-stone. You clear up dreams for those who live in fog."

Denvy shook his head. "You give me far too much credit."

She scoffed and waved her hand, dismissing his low murmur. She pointed across the burning-sea, to the tall, glistening spires protruding from the dunes.

"Those are the Rythrya Stones. The Tall Mirrors."

Jythal's paw sought her shoulder to steady himself. "How do you know? Few have ever seen the Rythrya Stones."

"At the Iposti Haven Hall, where I was raised, many scrolls depicted what they looked like." Nixlye plucked at the blanket across her lap. "I gather the Rythrya are different to the guiding stones Aaldryn speaks of?" Denvy asked.

"The guiding stones are used by wind chaplains, like Aaldryn, as guides to gauge the currents," Jythal said. "However, the Rythrya themselves, well, no one truly knows what they are, for they move with the currents of the burning-sea. Guiding stones remain stationary."

Denvy swept up a pawful of sand, letting it run over his pads. Utillia had once been an oasis of coral reefs, an ocean of great sea-weed forests, and, between those trunks of rippling, swaying green snakes that stretched to the heavens, gleaming Zaprex spires had soared. His people had lived side by side with the fairy race, contentedly and blissfully, merging iron cities with coral. Now all of that lay buried under an ocean of sand, but time could not swiftly erode that which a Zaprex built to last. Denvy studied the spires in the distance. They were too far for him to know for certain, but they had the distinct allure of a fairy castle.

"The Iposti speculate that the Rythrya Stones might even create the currents," Nixlye said.

Denvy's eyebrows lifted. "Really? Now that's something rather fascinating."

"It is?" Nixlye looked at him, surprised by his sudden surge in interest.

Denvy inclined his head in the direction of the spires as he scooped up another pawful of sand, throwing it into her lap. She growled playfully, brushing it from her tartan blanket. "The burning-sea is the result of a defunct desktop grid. All energy that had once been applied to the desktop of Utillia is now likely being channelled into the sky-sea." He pointed upwards. "The environmental system."

Jythal nodded slowly. "So, what then, is creating the currents if the desktop grid of Utillia is inoperative?"

Denvy opened his arms. "I imagine that is a question the Iposti have been asking for quite some time, yes?"

"True. Though the word amongst the Prides is that the Iposti have the charts that record the movements of the Rythrya Stones, but they keep them hidden, so that only they know where they are and where to lead the Wind Cities for good fortune." Jythal's paws twisted into fists, then slowly relaxed. His air-gills frilled out as he shook off all signs of frustration.

"That doesn't mean they have figured out what the Rythrya Stones are, though," Nixlye mused. "Aaldryn's been diving the cities for sol-cycles and he couldn't even begin to explain half of what he's seen. And he has an ancient wind-god living inside him."

"True, I suppose." Jythal sighed.

Denvy slowly rose to his foot-paws. He tugged on his gradually regrowing mane. A dream all misfits dreamt, a dream of spires that could never be found, that always called to the wandering souls of the burning-sea, as if calling to kindred spirits.

"Where did you think the Iposti keep these records?"

Jythal's grin was far too vindictive for the usually passive doctor. Denvy repressed a shudder. "If anywhere, they would be in one of the Haven Halls, upon the Wind Cities."

Nixlye tipped her head in his direction. "You can't seriously be thinking of trying to find the Rythrya Stones."

Denvy raised an eyebrow. "My dear, a mass dreaming on this scale, happening for centuries, and you expect me not to be curious about it to the point of wanting to discover what the source behind such power might be? Oh, we are very much going to find your Rythrya Stones."

Nixlye gripped Jythal's paw on her shoulder. "We're going on an adventure, dear."

Denvy turned away from the couple. On the horizon of the dunes, the large tail of a sand-sea creature had risen through the folds, spraying up sand. The rays pierced through the spray of particles like a shimmer of raining diamonds. As the golden Sun finally streaked the skyline in a full globe, a familiar azure glow he had known since he was a cub wrapped him a world of safety.

He was suddenly aware that he was standing alone in the dream-scape. Nixlye and Jythal had woken, most likely, leaving him with a hollow, vacant sensation lingering within his mind. His shoulders sagged and he tipped his head back. Would he be stuck in this desert until he woke? With the yoke still around his neck, how much control of his dreamathic skills did he truly have?

"Alone…" he whispered. "I am always alone."

"Who said anything about being alone, brother?" The wind carried the voice, but it was not Aaldryn's, nor the cultured monotones of Jythal. It was an echo within the dreamscape that gave the illusion of the owner of the voice being more distant than it was. The presence that was causing his fur to spike was nearby, and crafted purely of the fabric that formed the Secondary Realm—data. A mass of data, congested into a singularity. For a moment he feared it was the Dragon, but there was no crushing malice weighing him down.

"Ryojin." Denvy breathed out. "How are you…?" The rest of his words were simply lost on his dry tongue. The young prince stood a few paces away, admiring the sun on the spires in the distance. The rays shone through the tiny swirling blocks that formed his shape, creating a halo around his figure. Ryojin shrugged nonchalantly as he stepped closer.

"Apparently, according to System-Death, whom I just met by the way, to cross the Osiris Gate you need all of your data intact, or you'll end up corrupted when the cycle begins again."

Denvy's stomach twisted. He did not like where this conversation was heading.

"No one caught up in the null-zone can re-enter the mainframe. We can't pass the Osiris Gate." Ryojin looked at the blue sky-sea. "Everyone in Ishabal—my father, everyone—they're all gone. Their data is gone. It won't be restored, or reused, or anything. They're scattered junk." He frilled out his air-gills and looked at Denvy. "I caught the tail end of the null-zone, just enough for it to corrupt some data, but not enough to—"

"Destroy your avatar. I know." Denvy shook his head. "I'm sorry."

"It's not your fault I'm dead, brother." Ryojin smiled. "Besides, I just met System-Death. The System of Death! He asked me what I would like to do, since I can't pass the Osiris Gate. I could become one of his Jackals, but that wasn't particularly appealing, so I asked if there was any way in which I could help those I've left behind."

Ryojin's tail twirled across the sand. "He told me I was being audacious. That, right now, the Secondary Realm is a dangerous place for wandering data."

"It is." Denvy crouched, again scooping up a pawful of warm sand. As realistic as it felt, it was no more real than the avatar of the prince who stood beside him. Ryojin had become an accumulation of songs that would gradually dissipate over time. A swift death would have been far kinder in his opinion. The fragmenting of a song that had once been an entity within the Primary Realm was like witnessing a gradually cracking plate.

"Just because something is dangerous doesn't mean you resist it," Ryojin continued. "So, here I am."

Denvy dusted off his paws. "I am still not entirely sure where here is, or how I came to be here. I shouldn't be capable of logging into the Secondary Realm in my current condition."

"Don't be ridiculous. Even with that yoke, you're the strongest Dream Master in the Northlands."

Denvy's tail went deathly still. He had no recollection of mentioning who, or what, he was to the young prince upon their first meeting. He stole a glance his way, his brow furrowing. There was no malice that he could sense. The avatar was not a virus, come to claim his data, nor was it the Dragon—that much he would have known instantly. The Dragon would never have been so fickle as to trick him.

"How do you know who I am? Or even about the yoke?"

Ryojin gave him a scrupulous look. "You are aware that I am now, in a manner of speaking, part of the same system you are. I have all the information the Secondary Realm contains."

Denvy scratched the bridge of his nose. "Of course, of course."

"Denvy." Ryojin's paw touched his arm. "The yoke is only preventing you from accessing your dreamathic skills; it hasn't taken them away. You are still the Dream Master of the Northlands. You are still the Mapmaker."

He pulled away from the younger prince, staring down at him in frigid horror. He had not heard himself referred to by his executable filename in eons. The urge to run surged through his legs, but he tightened his muscles and bit down on his lower lip. Sharp pain caused his ears to flick and he looked away, shamefully, from the young prince.

"Think of me as a shortcut, or a bypass." Ryojin took up his paws, squeezing them. "A way around the yoke restricting you. Denvy, use me as your link between the Realms."

"You did this? You brought me into this dreamscape."

"You're my connection now to Nixlye and Jythal, old man. You're going to be stuck with me until such a time as my data disperses beyond usefulness." The eyes that stared up at him swirled with songs, the tiny little blocks that formed the avatar he could see, spinning around, as though they were stars within a galaxy. Denvy cupped Ryojin's cheek, ignoring the crackle of energy that sparked between them.

"Even with your help, I seriously doubt I could be the Mapmaker again. I have not been that program in a long time."

"Then what can you do?"

"I might not be able to ride the Data-Ways yet, however I am a Dream Master, and this is a dream." He chuckled low in his chest, brushing a paw through the folds of his air-gills. A tingling beset his foot-paws as he spoke, and a surging ring of hexagons spilled out, vanquishing the dreamscape surrounding them.

"I desire twenty barrels of Mist."

From a ground now made of starlight, tiny bricks began shifting into place, crawling over each other to form gleaming shapes that solidified into brown, wooden kegs, smelling of fine, cooked rice. Ryojin's laughter erupted through the galaxies twirling around them.

Denvy spread a paw wide. "When I wake, they will be placed within the brig of the *Lawless Child*." He looked at Ryojin. "And you will be a data-crystal, in the palm of my paw."

Ryojin had barely a moment to gasp in surprise as his avatar split, scattering into thousands of pixels. Denvy clicked his claws a few times, in the old manner he was familiar with, yet something he had not done in sol-cycles. "Awaken."

Dreaming always caused insomnia. It was a strange contradiction. Despite his exhaustion and muscle ache from fleeing the collapsing streets of Ishabal, and struggling against the pull of the burning-sea,

Denvy felt compelled to pace the corridors of the *Lawless Child*. There was a sorrowful silence cast over the sand-ship, a respectful pall. The crew were in mourning for the souls who had been sucked into the depths below the surface. A whole city lost. It was a tragedy, far more so than they could truly grasp. Songs unable to pass beyond the Osiris Gate: it made his head heavy with the thought of such waste. Nixlye's sorrow had left an imprint on his mind from their shared dream, lingering like the trails of a shredded fabric. She had been weeping for her lost friend, gone so suddenly, without hope of a goodbye. He fingered the indigo crystal in his paw, warm to the touch, humming with the song stored within it. Should he tell the young queen about Ryojin, to uplift her spirits? Or would it create greater despair for her to know the eventual fate of her friend? Attaching the crystal to the strap that held the geode, he tucked the necklace back under the yoke, and steeled himself for the cold wind beyond the warmth of the *Lawless Child's* corridors.

The silence continued outside, in the darkness of the night. Mist radiated through sails glowing a soft heat that tickled his fur, causing his air-gills to expand. A skeleton crew moved in the shadows, tending to the creaking sand-ship under dancing starlight.

Denvy leant wearily against the railing, moving with the tip and sway of the vessel. The burning-sea shimmered, the dunes lit with a reflection of the Twin Moons and the blanket of stars adorning the night sky-sea. It was an alien land. His mind refused to see it as Utillia. Utillia was as he remembered it. A lush land, atmosphere so thick one could swim through it. It had been toxic to Humans and Kelibs; home only to Kattamonts and Zaprexes. He had loved the deeper regions of the ancient coral forests, even more toxic, where dangerous flora and fauna dwelt. They—the Kattamonts—had built their homes in the high corals, bouncing on the clouds. He could recall swimming with a school of ewnnins, or as Hazanin-*sama* had called them, 'dolphins', in honour of a similar creature from its home world, the little blue planet.

Now all that surrounded him was shifting, burning sand—his true home was buried. Had it become nothing but dust?

"You wouldn't happen to have anything to do with the twenty extra kegs of Mist in the hold, would you?" Zafiashid's voice startled him. He had not sensed her presence nor smelt her approach. Denvy touched his chest, frowning at the crackle and pop of the Human illness still coating his lungs and nostrils. It was flaring up again. Here he had thought the worst was over. Maybe he had taxed himself with twenty barrels.

Flicking his tail, Denvy shrugged. "Perhaps."

In the twin moonlight, the queen's reflective eyes studied him, and she responded with a scowl, somewhere between motherly concern and irritation for his lack of definitive reply.

"I didn't want to believe it," she huffed out. "You really are *that* old."

Denvy tugged on the tufts of his mane. "Well, when you say it like that."

"No, no." She waved a paw. "I mean…" Zafiashid sighed, her teeth gritting together. "I am not like my son, nor even like his mate and blood-brother. I have never believed much in what lies beneath the sands. What I see is what I get. I can't defeat enemies I cannot rip my claws into." She pointed to his chest. "But you are something of an enigma."

He chuckled, only for the laughter to turn into a rasping cough. Zafiashid stepped forward, but hesitated, her lips turning down.

"Bother," he griped.

"You should not be out of bed." Zafiashid sat down on a crate, clicking her tongue in disproval. "That Human illness will be the death of you."

"I'm just restless. Besides, the sky-sea is beautiful."

"Jythal will disapprove of your wandering."

He had a feeling it was she who disapproved of his wandering, but that she was using the excuse of the doctor to guilt him back to bed. It was not going to work. He had no desire to return to the land of dreams just yet.

Denvy raised his brow. "Your confidence in your princess's mate is comforting. If I recall, mature queens such as yourself rarely sought the company of youthful Prides."

Zafiashid snorted. She swept her tail across her lap. "And here I thought I was young."

"To your own people, my dear, you have seen many things that makes you old."

A brief smile graced her lips at his words, before she ducked her head away, like a shy cub.

"They are your people as well." Her paw fleetingly brushed his arm.

Denvy shook his head. "I am afraid I am not that much of a Kattamont anymore."

"It will come back to you, old one."

"You know, you are very welcome to just call me Denvy." He turned, though every muscle protested the movement as he faced her, taking in the subtle changes of her features. She was not dreamathic. It was impossible to even begin to sense her emotions with the yoke binding his mind. But, strangely enough, it heightened every little movement, every twitch of her whiskers and flick of her ears. The light of the Mist through the sails made her dark pelt shine and the spectral sheen of her feathers illume, evoking the ancestry she could rightly claim lineage to—she was a true Silvertide Queen.

"Tell me," he asked, scratching at his chin, "how did a queen such as yourself end up the lone warrior and captain of a single small trading sand-ship that houses outcasts and misfits?"

The defiant shine in her eyes dulled with grief. Her claws plucked at her fan-tail feathers. "Perhaps, Denvy, someday I shall tell you the sad tale." She unfolded from the crate and brushed past him to stand beside him at the railing. She was small against him. She would have been small compared with most princes, and many princesses, but it felt comfortable as she slotted in beneath his arm.

"For now I will simply tell you that I disagreed with how my Pride treated those they considered inferior." Zafiashid sniffed. "The princesses thought that by casting me out I would die without a Pride, for they knew none of them could defeat me in battle." Her brow furrowed. "But my Pride is the dancing stars, the grains in the burning-sea, and all the ghosts of the slain misfit children I could not save. I have my Pride."

He reached for her paw, smothering it in his own and squeezing it tightly. "You are a true queen."

Her smile was hesitant, and beautiful, stealing his breath from his lungs.

"And you, old one, are Utillia's Gold Lion. I am glad you have returned to your Pride."

His pride. Utillia was his pride. He had never been a part of Utillia, nor the Kattamont nation—but perhaps this time it would be different. Denvy turned to the gleaming dunes and the sorrowful song on the tongue of the wind. "Something has gone dreadfully wrong and I intend to find out what that is." He squeezed her paw again. "Will you help me, Queen Zafiashid Silvertide?"

"I feel the tides changing," she whispered.

SEKHMET OF THE NORTHERN TOWER

NEFERTEM THE PROGRAMMER

Trench Ealdo

Myths of the Messengers

KYLIE LEANE

About the Author

Kylie Leane lives in the beautiful hills of Adelaide, South Australia, with her dimensional hopping pet cat Aislinn Dreamer. When they are not travelling to different worlds, recording historical events, she spends a considerable amount of time at the local café writing, and in her spare time she illustrates cute little green aliens, or watches some Anime (update on the Netflix situation, dimensional rift has moved - now have access.)

Having been raised with a love of old classic Science Fiction thanks to her Dad, Kylie adores all things spacey and science and she acquired a bountiful amount of creativity thanks to her resourceful Mum.

Kylie started writing *Chronicles of the Children* when she was about ten, coming up with the idea for the story in the back seat of the car on a long drive with the family. Despite being dyslexic, she taught herself how to write and spell through her stories.

Kylie was diagnosed with chronic pain when she was nineteen, and now tries to live life day to day. She's come to realize that she is going to be in pain anyway, so she may as well live her life to the best of her abilities. She had always found strength in the world of imagination and story-telling, and uses her weaving of tales and characters as a way to cope with the daily battle of pain.

She has a great desire to share her stories with the world and to spend her life encouraging others to use their own gifts. To let them know that even though they might have their own limitations, through their own imagination and their uniqueness everyone has a truly marvelous and incredible strength living inside them.

Due to her chronic pain, Kylie tends to spend many hours inhabiting little corners of the world wide web, such as Facebook and Youtube.
She loves hearing from people, so if you ever happen to be online feel free to drop her a line—she has a website, blog and email:

authorkylie.com

authorkyileleane@gmail.com

BINARY/HEXADECIMAL TO TEXT

Chapter Two:
Sekhmet

Chapter Six:
Do not speak of the Key so freely. They could be listening.

Chapter Ten:
Send Beer

Chapter Twelve:
I have the Key. Safe. Kemet/Cal'pash'coo. Finding Osiris.
Last Transmission. Hazanin.